Dr Patras was glaring down at her.

'I need an administrative sister who can cope with her work. I think the way you were appointed was highly irregular.'

'And how exactly were you appointed, Doctor?' asked Pippa.

'That's different. Alexander needed a favour from me, and——'

'And Nicole needed a favour from me. And as far as the work goes, you've no need to worry. I'll do the work if it kills me.'

'And it probably will!' he flung at her.

Dear Reader

NEVER PAST LOVING is Book Two of Margaret O'Neill's quartet, which has more of an administrative setting, and we launch the first of two books by Marion Lennox. A LOVING LEGACY involves general practice in outback Australia; you'll love Richard and Kate's battles. Next month, Richard's sister Christy will be our heroine. FALSE IMPRESSIONS by Laura MacDonald explores occupational nursing, and Margaret Barker returns to Ceres Island again, first met in her OLYMPIC SURGEON several years ago. This time, in SURGEON'S DILEMMA, Nicole's cousin Pippa is the heroine. Happy New Year!

The Editor

Margaret Barker pursued a variety of interesting careers before she became a full-time author. Besides holding a BA degree in French and linguistics, she is a Licentiate of the Royal Academy of Music, a state registered nurse and a qualified teacher. Happily married, she has two sons, a daughter and an increasing number of grandchildren. She lives with her husband in a sixteenth-century thatched house near the sea.

Recent titles by the same author:

RED SEA REUNION
HIGHLAND FLING

SURGEON'S DILEMMA

BY
MARGARET BARKER

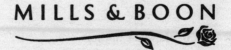

MILLS & BOON

MILLS & BOON LIMITED
ETON HOUSE, 18–24 PARADISE ROAD
RICHMOND, SURREY, TW9 1SR

*First published in Great Britain 1994
by Mills & Boon Limited*

© Margaret Barker 1994

*Australian copyright 1994
Philippine copyright 1994
This edition 1994*

ISBN 0 263 78438 X

*Set in 10 on 12 pt Linotron Times
03-9401-52233*

*Typeset in Great Britain by Centracet, Cambridge
Made and printed in Great Britain*

CHAPTER ONE

As THE boat rounded the headland the view of Ceres Harbour took Pippa's breath away. She was totally unprepared for the fascinating kaleidoscope of pastel colours that assaulted her senses. Ancient buildings painted pink, blue, green, white, their red roofs shining in the sunlight, tumbled down from the top of the majestic mountain slopes, their picturesque descent ending at the edge of the dazzling blue sea. Small fishing boats jockeyed for position, sometimes double-parked along the quayside. Taverna doors, open wide, or non-existent, exuded a friendly welcome and from somewhere along the narrow streets beside the harbour came the sound of a bouzouki player, accompanied by the steady rhythm of a drum.

So this was Ceres, the island where she was to work for six months. From first impression, that would be no hardship! This appeared to be Pippa's kind of island. And yet cousin Nicole had hinted in her letter that Ceres was not all it seemed in a superficial appraisal. Nicole had written,

> The tourists come and go, but they only see what they want to see. They enjoy their two weeks' holiday and then leave. But you, Pippa, if you agree to come out, will find a different Ceres, because you will be working among the people. And in the hospital the patients will open their hearts to you and you will have to allay their fears. I found it hard

when I came out here as a young nursing sister eight years ago. But I fell in love and married Alexander, so my early memories are now rose-tinted. We have a wonderful marriage and I'm blissfully happy. Before the children came I used to help Alexander at the hospital. . .

Pippa leaned over the side of the boat as she remembered Nicole's letter, the letter that had changed her life so quickly. It was a letter that had come in reply to her own. Funny how she always wrote to Nicole when life was difficult. She supposed it was because Nicole had been like a big sister to her when she was small. Being eight years younger than she was, it was only natural that she should look up to her, and when Nicole had gone off to train as a nurse the idea had been planted in Pippa's head that this was a worthwhile, interesting career. She'd watched Nicole making progress and decided that as soon as she was old enough she'd follow Nicole to the Benington General on the outskirts of London.

She'd missed her cousin when Nicole had married and gone to live with her consultant husband on this idyllic Greek island. Looking out across the water towards it now. Pippa could see what a wonderful life Nicole must have. She hadn't known much about it when she'd written to her cousin telling her about the injury to her foot.

It had been such rotten luck, stepping on that wretched glass bottle last Christmas morning when she had run into the tarn with her brothers before their annual Christmas swim. She remembered how the water had been so cold that they were surprised it wasn't frozen over. Her older brothers, Simon and

Peter, had been dragging her in, laughing at the way she was shivering, and she'd decided she would show them just how tough she was. So she'd run headlong towards the deeper water and stepped on a broken bottle. . . Would she ever forget the pain that had seared up her leg?

She shivered now, in spite of the warm sunlight, remembering how she'd written to Nicole describing the event and explaining that old Dr Marsh in the village had bound up her foot and told her to rest after he'd removed the bits of glass. What a Christmas Day that was! But the worst had been yet to come. Three months afer the event Pippa's foot had started swelling up and feeling painful. The RMO in the nurses' sick-bay had got her X-rayed and it had appeared that there were small slivers of glass deeply embedded in the foot. Several days as a patient in hospital and an operation to remove the glass had been followed by two weeks on crutches. But the worst part, she'd told Nicole in her letter, was being put on light duties in the records office. After running her own surgical ward for the past couple of years, this was too much. She'd asked Nicole,

> Can you imagine how bored I get? I don't know how much longer I can stand it, but the RMO insists that the foot has been weakened due to having the glass in it for so long. It was suffering from Sudek's atrophy, apparently, and only time will build up strength in the bones and the surrounding structure.

The replying letter from Nicole had been like a ray of sunshine.

> I've got the perfect solution, Pippa! How about six months on Ceres? Alexander and I have to go to

the States for a six-month lecture tour. We'd like to
take our administrative sister with us. Now
Alexander could appoint someone from within the
hospital, but doesn't feel there's anyone suitable.
We could advertise and get a total stranger, or you
could come out and take the post. Heaven knows
you're well qualified enough! I know you'd love it
out here and you could keep an eye on Alexander's
father for us. He's a real sweetie and he misses us
and his grandchildren so much when we're away.
You'd only have to visit occasionally and keep him
up to date with the hospital gossip—I believe I told
you he founded the Ceres Hospital and still helps
out financially. Do say you'll come, because here
you'll be your own boss, able to put your feet up
when necessary, and the pace of life on Ceres is so
slow that. . .

Pippa looked down at the fish swimming in the clear
blue water of the harbour as she remembered. She'd
been convinced, long before she reached the end of
Nicole's letter, that this would be the perfect solution.
She would look upon it as a working holiday, and
when the six months was up she'd return to the
Benington, fighting fit, and ready to continue her
exacting work as a ward sister.

The boat was only yards from the shore now. A
dark, swarthy Greek sailor in a blue shirt and jeans
was leaning on an iron post set firmly on the quayside.
Standing beside him was a tall, dark-haired man wearing stone-coloured denim trousers and a white cotton
polo shirt open at the neck to reveal the thick dark
hairs of his tanned chest, which mingled with the
stethoscope slung casually around his neck.

Pippa surmised that this must be one of the doctors from the hospital, come to meet her. She took a deep breath to steady her nerves. The doctor was obviously Greek, very good-looking in a tanned Mediterranean sort of way, the sort of man she'd seen in films where the heroine fell madly in love on a hot, sandy beach and the hero scooped her into his arms. She was sure his teeth would be strong and white. . .but the man on the quayside wasn't smiling, so she had no way of confirming her light-hearted fantasy. In fact, come to think of it, he was positively glowering up at the boat, his eyes scanning the faces of the passengers until they came to rest on hers.

'Are you Sister Manson?' he called impatiently.

The other passengers turned to look at her. However did he know? She wasn't in uniform. The white shirt and blue denim skirt couldn't be mistaken for hospital issue, she hoped. So Nicole must have given the doctor a description of her. It would have said: dark, shoulder-length hair, age twenty-five, medium height. . . She leaned over the side. 'Yes, I'm Sister Manson. And you must be —— '

'Do you think you could get a move on? I'd like to get back to the hospital,' came back the inhospitable reply.

Pippa muttered under her breath, 'And welcome to Ceres!' This wasn't what she'd imagined. This self-important man was probably the friend of Alexander's who'd come to fill in for six months, as she had. But he couldn't have a very important job if he could take time off to languish on a primitive island where nothing much happened. She'd soon put him in his place!

Carefully she began to negotiate the ridged wooden gangplank. Since the foot injury she'd taken extra care, because her balance wasn't quite right yet. She wanted to look up and see if the arrogant doctor was still watching her, but the effort of pulling her case on wheels and making sure she didn't fall required all her attention.

She reached the bottom rung. There! She relaxed and looked up as she stepped on to the quayside.

Wham! The pain seared up her left leg again. Oh, God! She'd stubbed her toe on one of the uneven stones and the pain was excruciating. But she dared not cry out. First impressions were so important, she thought as she fell forwards, literally into the arms of the unwelcoming doctor.

'What on earth do you think you're doing?' The dark-haired man held her away from him at arm's length, his fingers digging into her flesh.

She grimaced. 'I've hurt my foot,' she muttered between clenched teeth.

'So I was told, and I may say that I don't approve of the way you've been foisted upon me.'

'But I've just hurt it again,' she said, in a barely audible hoarse whisper.

The doctor glanced down at Pippa's foot, where the obvious signs of swelling were beginning to show between the straps of her orthopaedic walking sandals. He let out an exasperated sigh.

'This is all we need. Why didn't you take care when getting off the boat? As soon as I heard about the Sudek's atrophy in your foot I tried to cancel your contract. But you'd already left. I'd better get someone to call the ambulance down from the hospital.'

He spoke quickly in Greek to one of the young men on the quayside, who nodded and ran up the steps to the white hospital building that looked out to sea over the roofs of the tavernas and shops that clustered beside the water.

'Meanwhile, you'd better sit down,' he added, grudgingly, putting an arm around her waist and urging her towards a chair outside the nearest harbourside taverna. 'You'd better hop. Don't put any weight on that foot. You might have broken a bone.'

'But it was only a slight knock just now. I don't think——'

'With Sudek's atrophy you could have done anything to it,' he snapped. 'Your foot has been severely weakened due to the trauma of the glass being embedded in it for so long. . . Oh, yes, I've read your notes. I know all about you. We'll have to get that foot X-rayed as soon as we get up to the hospital.'

She was perched on the edge of an uncomfortable wooden chair, looking out across the water. She tried to concentrate on the activity going on around her, so as to dispel her anxiety and take her mind off the pain. Supposing she really had broken a bone. . . Oh, no, please, no! How would she cope with the new job if. . .?

She took a deep breath as she told herself she must be positive about this. Deliberately she tried to stop thinking about herself as she watched a young boy hauling a basket of live lobsters across the cobblestones into a taverna. Two men, alighting from a sponge boat, began beating and washing sponges. The tourists from Pippa's boat who'd crowded around her were now quickly dispersing, anxious to make the most of their day trip to this fascinating, unspoiled island.

The doctor leaned down and began to remove her sandal. His fingers were gentle, but the pain seared up her leg again as he uncovered her foot. She stared down at the swelling. This was not how she'd planned to create an impression on Ceres!

She could hear the ambulance tearing down the narrow road behind the taverna, skirting the hairpin bend and clattering over the cobblestones to stop a couple of yards from Pippa's chair.

She was being lifted inside by a couple of Greek hospital porters.

'Gently, gently,' the doctor remonstrated.

Well, at least he's human! Pippa thought fleetingly as she bit back the cry that threatened to escape her lips.

'I don't know your name,' she said as the doors clanged to, leaving her to the mercy of the impatient doctor.

'Adonis Patras,' the doctor replied brusquely. 'Alexander persuaded me to take over for six months. I'm beginning to regret helping him out. Now stop prattling and conserve your strength, woman!'

Prattling! she thought viciously. She'd hardly spoken two words in the time she'd spent with this ogre. . . albeit a good-looking ogre. The man didn't deserve to be so handsome. Imagine going out with him on the strength of his outward appearance and then discovering how dreadful he really was! At least he'd shown his true colours to her right from the outset.

She winced as the porters helped her into a wheelchair. Glancing upwards, she saw the impatient but resigned look on the doctor's face.

'You have such a wonderful bedside manner, Doctor,' she said quietly, not caring whether he heard her or not.

The deep brown eyes narrowed as Dr Patras bent his head towards her.

'I save myself for the real patients,' he muttered. 'I've no sympathy for ailing nursing sisters who're looking for a soft option.' He turned his head and smiled at the young Greek nurse who was accompanying them. 'We're going to X-Ray, Nurse. How are you enjoying working here? This is your first year, I believe.'

The young Greek woman smiled back at this delightful addition to the medical staff. All the nurses were beginning to swoon at his charms. . .but not this newly arrived English sister, from the look of things.

As Dr Patras chivvied the X-ray staff into moving quickly Pippa lay still on the examination couch, almost holding her breath with apprehension. Surreptitiously she glanced around her, hoping that no one could see just how worried she was. Supposing. . .yes, just supposing she'd chipped a bone. . . And it could have happened; heaven knew, it was painful enough! What would she do then?

After what seemed like an eternity, the resultant X-rays were held up to the light. Dr Patras frowned and held them towards Pippa.

'You can see the thinning of the bone, which is typical of Sudek's atrophy. But you haven't cracked anything.'

Pippa let out an involuntary sigh of relief as the irascible doctor continued his diagnosis.

'A slight displacement of the big toe here. . . Your tendons need strengthening. This sort of thing is bound to happen when you're careless, and it's going to set you back a few weeks every time you do something silly.'

'I do not do silly things on purpose, Dr Patras,'
Pippa put in icily. Now that she knew there was no
fracture she began to feel optimistic again. Her work
as administrative sister couldn't possibly be as physically demanding as running her own surgical ward at
the Benington. Nicole wouldn't have suggested she
come out if she didn't think she could cope. Pippa had
absolute faith in her cousin's judgement. This latest
injury was only a slight setback. So long as she could
avoid too much strain on the injured foot for a few
days the pain should subside, and she would gradually
become more and more mobile.

Dr Patras was glaring down at her. 'You came out
here. That was one of the silliest things to do. I need
an administrative sister who can cope with her work,
not a parasite planning to spend half her time in her
office with her feet up. I don't know what Nicole was
thinking about when she asked you out here. And
that's another thing. I think the way you were
appointed was highly irregular. The post should have
been advertised.'

'And how exactly were you appointed, Doctor?'
Pippa asked.

'That's different. Alexander needed a favour from
me, and——'

'And Nicole needed a favour from me. And as far
as the work goes, you've no need to worry. I'll do the
work if it kills me.'

'And it probably will!' he flung at her.

She looked around the empty X-ray room, relieved
that the staff had had the good sense to get out before
the dispute became any more animated. This wasn't
doing her image any good at all. She was going to have
her work cut out to convince the staff that she could

be an asset to the Ceres Hospital. This had never been a problem before, because back at the Benington she had an excellent track record and she'd been able to rest on her laurels after her accident. But here they didn't know how she would cope with a further injury.

She raised herself on her elbows and looked along the examination couch as Dr Patras bent to put a crêpe bandage on her foot.

'Keep still!'

She winced at the touch of his fingers and thought that the trouble with the foot was that there were so many different nerves involved. Taking a deep breath, she decided to put him straight on a few matters.

'You may as well accept the fact that I'm here for the next six months and we'll be working together.'

'Not if I can help it!'

'There's nothing you can do about it.'

'Oh, yes, there is. I shall request a replacement. I shall say you're not up to the job, which you plainly aren't.'

'My cousin Nicole's father-in-law, Dr Demetrius Capodistrias, is the founder of this hospital and chairman of the governors. He would turn down your request.'

'Nepotism!' he snarled, his lip curling in disgust.

'Perhaps,' Pippa conceded. 'But I'll show you I can do the job.'

They glared at one another, each sizing the other up.

The doctor pulled himself to his full height as he towered above her. 'I think you'd better go round to Symborio Bay and discuss the situation with Dr Demetrius. Alexander told me, just before he left on his lecture tour, that his father is hoping you'll go over

and spend your first night there. Dr Demetrius misses
Alexander and Nicole when they're away and regards
you as a family link. But I've already told him how I
feel about having an invalid foisted upon me, and he
wants to assess the situation himself. So while you're
there I'd like you to discuss with him whether he thinks
you'll be able to cope—and it's not a bad idea if he
sees you as you are now,' he added, motioning to the
bandaged foot.

Pippa frowned. 'How will I get there?'

He handed her a stick. 'Take the weight with this.
I'll get someone to take you over to Dr Demetrius's
place in Symborio Bay. One of our doctors lives there.
And I'll arrange for your luggage to go with you in the
boat.'

'I'd actually rather settle in here first before going
over,' Pippa said quickly.

The doctor gave her a wry smile. 'I'm sure you
would, but, as I said, I'm not convinced you can do
the job. Discuss the situation with Dr Demetrius and
we'll take it from there. After you've talked things
over I'll get in contact with him and let him know how
I feel.'

He walked out of the room without a backward
glance. Pippa would have liked to hurl the X-rays after
him! That would certainly help to relieve the frustration she felt, but it wouldn't help to convince this
impossible man that she was fit to become administrative sister.

She took a few deep breaths before picking up the
stick and lowering her good foot to the floor. She'd
used a stick when she first came off the crutches, so
she knew the technique, but with the latest setback to
her foot she found the pain very unpleasant. Again,

she told herelf it would wear off. But she wasn't looking forward to her trip over the water to see Dr Demetrius. What a pity that Nicole and Alexander had already left for the States. She could have done with some moral support at a time like this. But maybe Nicole's father-in-law would be sympathetic towards her. Then again, he might dismiss her out of hand and send her packing back to England. . .which would please the high and mighty Dr Adonis Patras no end!

'Sister Manson?'

The quiet, cultured voice with only the trace of a Greek accent surprised Pippa. A tall young man had come into X-Ray while she was testing out her stick.

'Yes, I'm Sister Manson, and you're. . .?'

'I'm Dr Dominic Varios.' The young man smiled, displaying white, even teeth. 'Dr Patras asked me to take you round to the Capodistrias family home. Let me help you.'

Once more, she was helped into an ambulance, whick took them down to the quayside. She leaned heavily on the young doctor's arm as he helped her into the waiting boat, making an effort to ignore the pain.

The engines roared into action and they were off, speeding across the blue water, leaving a wide curve of white-foamed wash behind them. The distinctive smell of the water titillated her nostrils. There was a hint of freshly caught fish mingling with the aroma of the herbs on the nearby hills. She caught a glimpse of a man sitting on a rock, preparing an octopus for lunch. Not a pleasant sight! All that creamy fluid running down the rock into the blue sea! She turned away, thinking that it was better not to dwell on what happened to the creatures of the sea before they arrived on the table.

She looked across at the young man at the helm of the boat and wondered what place Dominic Varios had in the Capodistrias household. She knew from her cousin's letters that the Capodistrias family were fascinating people. Old Dr Demetrius Capodistrias had been a very successful shipping magnate until the age of thirty-four, before he had decided to read medicine and, after qualifying, to return to his birthplace so that he could be of service to the islanders. Nicole's husband Alexander Capodistrias had followed in his father's footsteps, but the hospital on Ceres was only one of his international medical interests. Alexander, after his medical training in London, had gone on to become a successful consultant there. It was when he had been asked to spend some time on Ceres to solve an international drug problem that he had met and married Pippa's cousin Nicole.

Dominic Varios suddenly turned and, leaving control of the boat to one of the young sailors, he moved towards Pippa.

'It will only take a few minutes to reach the house,' he said. 'How are you feeling?.'

She smiled. 'A bit shell-shocked, to be honest, and I'm dying for a shower. I'd hoped to be settling into my room at the hospital by now, but Dr Patras thought otherwise. You've got my case on the boat, haven't you?'

The young doctor smiled back. 'We have indeed. Dr Patras was adamant that we take it with us. Don't worry. You'll soon be over in the Capodistrias house having your shower.'

'Well, that's something to look forward to. Tell me, do you live at the Capodistrias house, Dr Varios?'

'Oh, please, call me Dominic. Yes, I am what you would call a jack of all trades in the Capodistrias family. I was born in the house. My mother is the cook. My father works around the house and garden. I'm very lucky. The family helped me financially so that I could have a good education and go on to medical school. I qualified as a doctor last year, so I now work at the hospital. Today I'm off duty. It's a very fine hospital. Dr Demetrius Capodistrias planned and financed the building of it and he continues to help fund the day-to-day running of the place. We are very lucky on this island to have the Capodistrias family.'

They were rounding the headland and a new bay spread out before Pippa's eyes.

'Symborio Bay,' Dominic said, unable to disguise the pride and warmth he felt for his birthplace.

The next moment his voice changed as his fingers gripped the side of the boat. 'Look at those idiots fooling about in the water. The bay is too deep to mess about like that. The hill shelves straight down and. . .'

But he didn't finish his sentence. It had become obvious that the couple in the water were no longer fooling around. The young woman was having difficulties and the man was trying to life-save. The girl's cries were muffled as she went under the water again.

'Help!' The man waved one hand in the air while trying to support the girl with the other.

Kicking off his leather sandals, Dominic dived straight over the side of the boat and swam with swift, strong strokes towards the couple. Pippa watched anxiously. She could see Dominic directing the man to swim towards the boat, where the sailor had cut the engines. Dominic, after an initial struggle, had managed to pull the girl over on to his chest and was swimming backstroke, nearing the boat.

'Oh, thank God!' Pippa leaned over the side, her own pain forgotten as she stretched her arms towards the hapless man. Dominic and the girl reached the boat seconds later.

At first the girl appeared lifeless. One of the sailors helped the man to go below while Pippa and Dominic tried to revive the girl.

'Let's roll her on to her side,' Pippa said. As she moved the girl over there was a rush of frothy fluids on to the deck, which was what Pippa had hoped to achieve. Having ensured that there was no obstruction to the air passages, she pinched the girl's nosrils and began mouth-to-mouth resuscitation.

She gave the first four inflations of the chest in rapid succession to saturate the blood with oxygen. Then, raising her head, she was relieved to see that the chest had begun to rise and fall.

'I can feel her pulse. . .the heart's OK. . .but keep going, Sister,' Dominic said. He was still trying to regain his own breath after the exertions of the difficult life-saving swim. 'We'd best go back to the hospital.'

He spoke rapidly in Greek to the two sailors.

Seconds later the boat veered in an about-turn and headed back towards Ceres Town.

A crowd had gathered on the quayside. A radio message from Dominic had not only alerted the hospital but it appeared that the news of the emergency was spreading rapidly throughout Ceres Town. The ambulance that had delivered Pippa to the boat was back on the quayside again, looking strangely anachronistic amid the ancient buildings.

Pippa was relieved to find that her patient's breathing was becoming steadier. The girl's colour had improved and she'd been able to speak a few words, telling Pippa that her name was Gina.

Geoffrey, the young man, now wrapped in a blanket, was helped from the boat into the waiting ambulance. A stretcher was lowered for his girlfriend. Dominic helped Pippa from the boat and, using her stick, she made it under her own steam to the ambulance. The dull ache in her foot had been forgotten as she'd worked on her patient, but now it returned to nag her.

The doors of the ambulance closed and Pippa, sitting beside her patient, winced as she felt the vehicle hurtling up a short incline. In a matter of moments the ambulance doors were opened and they were being released in front of the low white-painted stone building, which blended in with the ancient buildings surrounding it.

A porter came out with a trolley to help Pippa and Dominic with Gina. A male nurse accompanied Geoffrey, still wrapped in a blanket, and they all went in through the wide main entrance to a cool reception area. A fan was whirring noisily in the ceiling overhead.

Pippa glanced down at her travel-weary denim skirt and crumpled white shirt. If only she'd had time to take that shower!

Her heart missed a beat as the impossible Dr Patras came through the swing-doors. If he noticed her he gave no indication as he bent down over Gina. Pippa stood quietly beside the stretcher as she watched the sensitive hands examining their patient while he talked in a gentle voice to allay the girl's fears — a completely different attitude from the way she'd been treated a short while before!

At length he raised himself to his full height and looked down at Pippa.

His eyes had a deeply caring expression. But beyond the doctor-patient concern was a fluid, stimulating look that disturbed and excited her.

'I have to admit you've done a good job here, Sister,' he said evenly. 'If you feel up to it, maybe you'd like to accompany our patient to her room and settle her in. We'll keep Gina in for a couple of days' observation, but I don't foresee any complications.'

The complications would be working with such a difficult man, Pippa thought, as she nodded, at last in agreement with the supercilious doctor. But she was determined that she would work with him whether he liked it or not. She was feeling stronger already and the pain in her foot was subsiding.

She glanced up at Adonis Patras as she desperately tried to keep up with him down the corridor. She realised that he'd slowed his impatient strides somewhat, but, even so, she knew she was still holding him back. But at least he wasn't commenting on the fact as they walked beside their patient along a white-painted corridor. His dark, handsome, aristocratic features gave nothing away. Suddenly he looked down at her and gave her a sardonic smile that displayed strong, even, dazzlingly white teeth.

'It may interest you to know that your cousin Nicole wrote up a glowing account of your career, Sister Manson. I doubt you would be able to live up to the reputation she's given you. But she told me all this before she mentioned your poor state of health. I was immediately wary of the situation and I told her so.

She asked me to judge for myself when you arrived whether or not you were up to the job. I gave the matter a great deal of thought and came to the conclusion that you were unsuitable. I phoned London, but you'd left. When I came down to the harbour today it was to ask you to return, but the unfortunate incident with your foot forced me to postpone my decision. However, after what you've just done, I think maybe we'll have to give you the chance to show us what you can do, so I'll postpone judgement. If only you were in good health you would be an asset to the hospital.'

Pippa's spirits soared, but she tried not to show it. She was determined that the doctor shouldn't think he could pick her up and put her down at whim. She didn't want him to assume she was a push-over and that he could walk right over her if he chose.

'Please don't patronise me, Dr Patras. My nursing career has——'

'Your nursing career has flourished, according to Nicole. . .and according to your c.v. and references,' the doctor interrupted in a bland voice. 'So there's no need for you to elaborate. You were top of your year in your finals and then went on to become the youngest sister at Benington General. Nicole seemed to think that you'd be able to cope here, but how do you know that Benington General will want to take you back after you've deserted them for six months and turned down their job in the records office? That couldn't have gone down too well.'

It hadn't, but Pippa wasn't about to admit this to him. 'Oh, there are other hospitals,' she replied airily. 'And who knows what might happen in the next six months?'

'Indeed. Six months is a long time.'

She looked down at the patient, who was still clutching her hand, and willed herself to remain calm and professional.

They went into a small room overlooking the sea. It had all the comforts of a bedroom, while still retaining the aseptic appearance of a hospital ward. The bed had a handle to crank up the mattress. When they had settled their patient in bed Dr Patras made the foot of the bed higher than the other end to ensure a good blood supply to the brain.

Pippa asked the Greek nurse who had accompanied them to close the curtains and observe Gina while she slept.

'We'll be back in a couple of hours when you've had time to rest,' Dr Patras told their patient.

The girl smiled gratefully and whispered her thanks as they left her.

'You seem to be handling your stick very well and walking OK; would you like me to show you round the hospital?' Adonis Patras asked Pippa.

She stared at him for a few seconds, trying to work out if this meant he was warming to the idea of accepting her. 'I would indeed. But what about Dr Demetrius? Isn't he expecting me?'

The dark eyes flickered momentarily. 'The arrangement was very fluid. Dr Demetrius is expecting you to go over some time today, but no actual time was specified. Greek hospitality is very easy going.'

So it would seem! Pippa thought. It seemed strange that, having been packed off to see Dr Demetrius before she'd even had time to settle in at the hospital, the arrangement was now postponed almost on the whim of this enigmatic doctor.

They were walking through into a large treatment-room in the centre of the building. Dr Patras paused, and Pippa leaned against one of the trolleys to steady herself.

'Tell me, Doctor, how many staff do we have here?' She deliberately used the word 'we' to outline the fact that she considered herself already a member of staff.

'I've only been here a week, so I'm still finding things out for myself. The staff situation seems to fluctuate, but basically I'm in control of the hospital while you will take charge of the administrative side of things, with particular reference to the nursing staff. There's a back-up team of four staff nurses, two night sisters, two day sisters, twelve part-time or full-time nurses, of which two are male, and four doctors. In addition there are several auxiliary nurses we can call upon if there is a staffing crisis.'

'And what nationality are all these people?'

'A good mix of Greek, English and Australian. The administrative sister from whom you're taking over is Greek. As you probably know, Alexander wanted her to accompany him to help with some of the lectures during his tour. I met her before they all left last week and she'll be a hard act to follow.'

'In what way?' Pippa asked quickly.

Adonis Patras gave a wry smile. 'Sister Arama was a perfectionist and terribly strict. The staff and patients were in awe of her, but she commanded great respect. Personally, I think everyone will welcome a more relaxed attitude. . .and you look as if you're a more easygoing person.'

Pippa didn't know whether to take this as a compliment. 'I may look relaxed now, but once I start work I can be pretty demanding if the nurses don't come up to scratch. My main concern is the patients' welfare.'

The doctor's dark brown eyes flickered. 'Are you planning to become one of those tyrant nursing sisters in your old age?'

Pippa smiled. 'Hadn't given it a thought. I'm only twenty-five, so there's a long way to go before I'm considered a dragon by the younger members of staff.' She moved away. 'Now tell me about this room,' she continued briskly. 'It's obviously the main treatment-room, with all those cubicles down the side, so where are the patients?'

'It may have escaped your notice, but it's actually lunchtime, and here on Ceres we take our midday break more seriously than you do in England. So might I suggest that we do a quick round of the hospital and then resume our discussion at one of the excellent tavernas down in the harbour?'

She was too stunned to reply.

'Oh, don't get any wild ideas, Sister. I simply want to sound you out and find if you really had thought you were coming out on a holiday or if you'd planned to do some work.'

'It may surprise you to know that I'd planned to and intend to work hard out here. The little setback this morning hasn't changed my plans in the slightest, but unless your attitude towards me changes I shall be forced to. . .'

'To what, Sister Manson?'

She hesitated. She'd been going to say she would resign, but that would be giving in to this high-handed man, and she'd be darned if she'd do that! She would ignore his taunts and do a good job, simply for the sake of the job, as she'd always done. He wanted her to resign, so she wouldn't give him the satisfaction.

'Actually, now you mention it, I realise I'm starving, so show me round the hospital and then you can take me for lunch.'

She enjoyed the baffled expression on the doctor's face as he began the tour. So this was the way to handle the great bully!

It was a small hospital, so the round didn't take long. Later on, when there was more time, she planned to go back and check everything out by herself, but for the moment she was content to glance inside the small operating-theatre at the back of the hospital. This was a cool room, built literally into the side of the hill, having been excavated from the rock. There was a large room which doubled as an out-patients section and casualty department leading off from the treat-ment-room. She had already seen one of the in-patient rooms, situated along the front and the side of the hospital, in which the patients were nursed. There were four single rooms, and four units shared out between obstetrics and gynaecology, surgical, medical and orthopaedic. But the movement of patients between the units was, of necessity, more fluid than in a large hospital.

'It's a cosy little hospital,' she said to Adonis Patras as they walked through the reception area and out into the bright sunshine.

'Tell me, what is this English word "cosy"? I've heard it before, but it seems to mean so many different things.'

'It's comfortable, small, inviting, welcoming. . .dif-ficult to explain, but this hospital has the same sort of feeling as the cottage hospital where I used to gain work experience when I was still at school.'

Dr Patras shook his head. 'I'm no wiser, but I'll take your word for it.'

It was difficult walking down the short, sloping road that led to the harbour front, but Pippa was determined not to show just how much the effort cost her. Dr Patras touched her elbow as he steered her towards the white-clothed tables in front of one of the tavernas. The feel of his fingers was unnerving in a peculiar, indefinable way. She didn't want him to touch her, and yet when he did the sensation was not unpleasant.

'Dr Patras!' One of the waiters rushed forward and began a rapid conversation in Greek while making a big display of finding the best harbourside table for them.

A glass of ouzo was placed in front of Pippa and she raised it to her lips. It looked innocuous enough and she was desperately thirsty after her long morning.

The doctor put out his hand to detain her, while calling for water. '*Nero, parakalo.*'

'Wait for the water,' Adonis Patras said, his dark, handsome face smiling. 'Ouzo is fiery stuff.'

He reached across to pour water into her glass. The colourless liquid became cloudy. 'Try it now,' he directed. '*Yasas!*'

'*Yasas!*' she echoed, remembering the Greek word, similar in meaning to the English 'Cheers!', from the language course she was working through.

Even though she was sipping gently the strong liquid seemed to scorch the back of her throat. She asked for some more water before trying again. All the while, she was aware of the dark, enigmatic eyes watching her across the table, the full-lipped mouth curved into an amused smile.

At length she raised her eyes to his and nodded her head. 'An interesting taste. . .but very refreshing when you're thirsty.'

'Good for you! I'm glad you're willing to try the local food and drink.'

A dish of olives had appeared on the table, flanked by a basket of fresh crusty bread and a plate of taramasalata, a Greek speciality made from fish roe. Pippa realised she was very hungry and helped herself while gently sipping the ouzo. The waiter was uncorking a bottle of white wine that sported the label Ilios. Adonis raised his glass towards her. 'I think I should give you a chance, so here's to a good working relationship, but I warn you——'

'And I warn you,' she cut in as she raised her glass towards his, 'don't put obstacles in my way. If you get on with your job I'll get on with mine. Don't worry about my health. It won't be a problem.' She only wished she felt as confident as her words!

Dr Patras drained his glass and set it on the table. 'I hope you're right. . .for your own sake and the sake of the patients.'

Pippa's pulses were racing. This man was the most disturbing character she'd ever met. Was it merely the challenge she was going for. . .or was there something else goading her on?

'You'll see,' she said quietly.

'I can't wait to see how you'll cope,' he said evenly, his eyes boring into her.

CHAPTER TWO

DURING the course of the meal Pippa sensed that they were both trying to remain emotionally detached — at least she was! She was determined to say nothing that would start up the animosity between them. But on the brief occasions when she was able to study this antagonistic doctor she was again struck by the fact that he was an extremely handsome man. His eyes, when they weren't spitting fire towards her, held a desirably fluid, warm, sensual expression that must endear him to staff and patients alike. And he probably thought, because of all the attention lavished upon him, that he was God's gift to women. Even his name, Adonis, reminded her of the myths and legends she'd learned about as a child. The mythical Adonis had been an exceptionally handsome youth, beloved of Aphrodite, the goddess of love. That had been one of Pippa's favourite myths.

Now, as she glanced across the table, she decided that it wasn't simply the stimulating, exciting expression in those eyes that made him obviously attractive to the opposite sex. No, it came naturally to Adonis Patras to turn on the charm when it suited him. And for the moment they seemed to be in a state of truce. She couldn't believe this charming man across the table was the ogre who'd scowled at her on her arrival. Oh, no! If he thought she was going to relax and put her guard down he was mistaken!

They were both trying to keep the conversation on

neutral ground, first of all discussing medical matters and then moving on to topical items in the world news, books and theatre — in fact anything that would continue to tone down this potentially explosive situation.

Pippa suddenly realised that an hour had elapsed over their lunch and they were still friends! Perhaps her initial fears were ungrounded. But then off-duty situations were different from professional ones and they had yet to work together. Still, it did no harm to find out if the man really was someone she would like to get to know.

'I'm intrigued by your name,' she said. 'The Adonis and Aphrodite story was one of my favourite Greek myths.

Dr Patras gave her a slight smile. 'The myth came initially from Babylon. But the story travelled westward and the Greeks made their own version.'

Pippa nodded. 'In the mythical version I read that the baby Adonis was so beautiful that the goddess Aphrodite determined to save him from destruction by hiding him in a casket which she gave to Persephone, goddess of the underworld. When Aphrodite returned to reclaim the casket she found that Persephone had opened it, seen the beauty of the baby, and decided to keep him herself. So Aphrodite appealed to the gods and Zeus decided that Adonis would spend half of each year on earth with Aphrodite and half in the underworld with Persephone.'

'Very good, Sister!'

She felt that he was patronising her and wished she hadn't started on this train of conversation. Better to keep their relationship strictly professional. Her foot was beginning to throb and she longed to put it up, but she wouldn't give him satisfaction by admitting the fact.

'That's why I'm here now,' Adonis Patras continued, with a whimsical smile. 'To spend the six months of spring and summer on this beautiful island. In the autumn I shall have to return to the streets of Athens and the colder, darker weather.'

'What do you do in Athens?' she asked quickly.

'I'm a professor of surgery. That's how I'm able to take six months off to help out my old friend Alexander. I was due for a sabbatical and it's good to get back into hospital work again. It's more satisfying than the academic life.'

So he did have an important job after all! she thought. He probably had all the female medical students swooning over his aristocratic good looks. No wonder he could choose to be so high-handedly super-cillious when it suited him. He must have been appalled at the idea of working alongside a twenty-five-year-old woman with an injured foot when he was used to the *crème de la crème* of healthy young girls.

'So tell me why your cousin Nicole calls you Pippa,' he broke in on her thoughts.

'It's short for Philippa.'

'I know. But I think Philippa is a much more beautiful name than Pippa. I can't see the point of spoiling a good name by creating an abreviation.'

The waiter came to remove the huge china fish plate complete with the remains of the *barbunia*, the red mullet, which had been so fresh and cooked to perfection. He gathered together the smaller plates that had held the *dolmades* — vine leaves — the green beans and the Greek salad.

Pippa heard Adonis ordering coffee and relaxed

against the back of her chair, easing her bandaged foot out of its sandal. Her thoughts turned to her patient, Gina, lying asleep at the hospital, and she soothed her professional conscience with the idea that a prolonged rest was the best treatment for the girl afer her near-drowning ordeal. There was no point in forcing a medical examination upon the patient when she was exhausted, and she was in good hands at the hospital. The ratio of staff to patients was certainly better than Pippa had ever experienced in London. If there was any change in Gina's condition, Adonis Patras would be immediately alerted on his bleeper.

Having quieted the feelings of guilt at spending so long over lunch, Pippa looked out across the blue water of the harbour to the other side of the town. The hillsides rose steeply from the water, giving the impression that the town was boiling away in a gigantic cauldron. The fishing boats on the water were still and calm in the early afternoon sun. Even the tourists had sought shelter from the hot May sunlight, positioning themselves under the brightly coloured umbrellas dotted along the harbourside tavernas. It had been only four hours by plane to Rhodes, then two hours by boat to Ceres, but Pippa felt she was a million miles from England.

Adonis Patras's deep, authoritative voice interrupted her thoughts. 'We've talked about the medical work on the island and the differences you'll have to cope with from your English work, but you've told me so little about yourself.'

'There's very little to tell, apart from what you've read in my c.v. and what Nicole has told you. Why don't you tell me about yourself and why you came to Ceres?'

She saw the surprise in his eyes and surmised that he hadn't expected her to be so bold. To be honest, she hadn't thought she could be so forceful with the man, but she'd realised that this was the only way she would impress him. . .and it had suddenly become very important to her that she do just that.

'I was actually born on this island,' he began. 'My family has a house here, near the Capodistrias residence over in Symborio Bay. I've known the Capodistrias family since I was a child. When Alexander telephoned me to say he wanted to go off on a lecture tour and asked if I could get away for six months to take his place, I jumped at the chance. I've been too long away from real medicine. It's good to get back to basics.' He glanced at his watch. 'It's time we were getting back to the hospital. How's the foot?'

'Fine,' she lied.

'You wouldn't prefer to take some time off?'

'Certainly not!' Wild horses couldn't force her to give in now that she'd glimpsed the man really did have human qualities. In fact she was finding him positively intriguing. If she could break down his initial distaste at her appointment she might enjoy working with him. She watched as he signalled to one of the waiters to bring over the bill. He had the cool confidence which came from a successful career and a well heeled background. But he also had an arrogant take-it-or-leave-it attitude that could be very disconcerting and impossible to break down. If he'd decided to give her a hard time professionally, then she would find the going tough.

He came round the table and stood looking down at her quizzically as she wriggled her foot into its unflatter-

ingly large sandal. 'The swelling's up,' he said evenly.
'You'll have to rest it.'

'Later, she said firmly. 'If it doesn't bother me, it
should be no concern of yours.'

'As you wish,' he said in a resigned tone. 'Let's go.'

He made no attempt to help her as she moved
between the tables, her hand gripping the stick to take
the weight off her bad foot. As she walked out on to
the uneven quayside she heard a high-pitched voice.

'Oh, how charming, Adonis. Do introduce me to
your friend.'

Pippa turned to find hereslf looking at a tall, slim,
impeccably dressed woman of indeterminate age. She
could have been twenty, thirty or even edging towards
forty. The high, aquiline Grecian features were
covered by a mask of flawless make-up, the skin
stretched taut over the perfect facial bone-structure.
The cream linen trousers and crimson silk shirt fitted
perfectly over her model-girl figure as she moved
swiftly through the tables on high, noisily clicking
heels.

If Adonis Patras was put out by the fashionable
vision he showed no sign of it, proceeding to effect the
introductions.

'Sister Philippa Manson, newly arrived from
England to take over as administrative sister at the
hospial. Cassiopi Manoulis.'

'How do you do, Sister Manson?' The woman held
out a well manicured hand. She glanced briefly at
Pippa's stick, but was obviously too well bred to
comment on the situation. As Pippa shook hands, she
noticed that there was no warmth in the eyes of this
woman.

'I tried to telephone you at the hospital, Adonis,'

Cassiopi said, quickly relinquishing Pippa's hand. 'They told me this was where I might find you. I need your advice. . .on a family matter.'

The doctor's face remained impassive. 'I have to go back to the hospital, Cassiopi. There's a new admission who needs checking out.'

Cassiopi spread out her hands in a gesture of impatience. 'But you have staff who can do that. Even young Dominic is capable of taking care of a new admission.'

'But I want to do this examination myself,' he replied, his tone crisp but courteous.

Cassiopi frowned, her glance turning from Adonis to Pippa. 'No doubt Sister Manson will be able to ease your task this afternoon. If you have time, Adonis, perhaps you would honour us with a visit this evening.'

She moved away as quickly as she had arrived. It was only then that Pippa noticed a dark blue Mercedes parked at the end of the quayside several yards away. The driver was standing beside the open passenger door, ready to help Cassiopi inside. The car moved off, weaving its way along the narrow harbourside towards the hill that led up to the old town.

'As I was saying, it's time to go back,' the doctor said, as if nothing had happened.

Pippa walked beside him up the uneven steps that led to the hospital road, hauling herself up on the handrail. 'What does Cassiopi do?' she asked, trying not to sound too out of breath.

'Do? Cassiopi doesn't have to do anything. . .except pass the time as agreeably as possible. The Manoulis family is very rich. They don't encourage their women to do anything outside the home.'

'Ah, so she's a married lady.'

'Not yet.'

The reply was brusque, indicating that Adonis Patras had no further wish to pursue the subject of Cassiopi.

A big cloud was passing over the sun, coinciding with the sudden chill that had cooled their relationship once more. The friendly interlude was over.

Pippa was intrigued by the proprietorial manner that Cassiopi had adopted with Adonis. This woman obviously meant something to him, she decided. But the relationship seemed one-sided — or perhaps Adonis Patras treated all his women with disdain. Yes, it was probably beneath him to show affection in public.

Back at the hospital, she accompanied the doctor to their new patient's room and found Gina was now awake. Pippa had put on a white coat, which would have to suffice until she could take a shower. She'd been informed that her sister's uniform had been delivered to her room in the medical quarters.

'How are you feeling, Gina?' Dr Patras asked, sitting down on the side of the bed.

The girl's face was very serious. 'I'm OK. . . I think . . .but then I haven't been too well recently. Doctor, would you examine me?'

'Of course. That's what I'm here for.'

'No, I meant would you check out my insides. . .? I think — in fact I know — I'm pregnant.'

'But why didn't you say something?' He leaned across and took hold of the patient's hand. 'My dear, if we'd known. . .'

'I didn't want anyone to know. . .not even Geoffrey . . .especially Geoffrey. You see, I was hoping I would lose it in the water. When I swam out to the middle of the deep bay today I was hoping I would be brave enough to end it all.'

Pippa leaned across their patient from the other side of the bed so that she and Adonis Patras were both holding one of the patient's hands. The girl's eyes were fixed on the white-painted ceiling as she spoke quietly but with intense calm.

'I'd decided I couldn't go through with it. We've no money, no jobs. Geoffrey's nineteen, I'm eighteen. I took out my savings from the post office and blew it all on tickets to this island. My parents used to bring me here when I was a child.'

'You're little more than a child now,' Dr Patras put in gently. 'How far on do you think you are?'

'About three months — maybe four. I've been starving myself so it wouldn't show. I thought if I had an accidental drowning no one would know about it. And Geoffrey wouldn't have me and the child depending on him. He's too young to get tied up with responsibilities. And it was all my fault because I forgot to take the Pill. He'd be furious if he knew.'

'No, he wouldn't!' Pippa said quickly, hoping that her assessment of the young man was correct. She'd only seen him briefly after he'd been settled in a bed in the medical unit for a few hours' observation, but he seemed like a kind, sensible person.

'Well, let's get on with this examination and then we'll decide what to do with you, young lady,' the doctor said briskly. 'We'll take you along to Obstetrics and check out what's going on.'

Gina was wheeled along to Obstetrics. Sister Ariadne Stangos was waiting for them, having been alerted over the internal phone system.

'We've come to do an examination, Sister,' Adonis Patras said. 'First we'd like to use the scanner.'

He went on to effect the introductions between the two sisters.

Sister Stangos gave Pippa a welcoming smile. 'So sorry to hear about your foot. How are you coping?'

'Oh, it's no problem,' Pippa said hastily, standing as upright as she could while surreptitiously relying heavily on the stick.

'So you're Nicole's cousin. I can see the family likeness, although you're much darker than she is.'

'Our mothers were sisters,' Pippa said. 'They were both fair-haired like Nicole, but I take after my father.'

Sister Stangos leaned against the desk. 'I remember the first day Nicole joined the hospital. She was very nervous. And Alexander gave her a bad time at first. If you ask me, I think it was only so that Nicole wouldn't know he'd fallen in love with her. But he didn't fool me. . . I could see right from the start that —'

'Is the scanner ready, Sister Stangos?' the doctor asked brusquely, turning around from the sink where he was scrubbing up.

The Greek sister smiled at Pippa. 'We must have a long chat some time. . .off duty,' she added as she saw the look on Dr Patras's face.

'I'd like that,' Pippa said, moving round to help their patient from the trolley.

'Now about this scan,' the doctor said briskly.

As soon as the scanner was switched on the image of the tiny foetus apeared on the screen.

'A healthy-looking foetus,' Adonis Patras observed. 'When was the date of your last period, Gina?'

Gina frowned. 'Difficult to say. My periods have always been irregular. Might have been the middle of January; could have been February. There was a slight show in February and I was keeping my fingers crossed it was a period. Then there was nothing in March and I started to worry. That was when I decided I couldn't go through with it. But I didn't dare go to my own doctor. He's an old friend of my dad's and I couldn't risk letting the family know.'

Dr Patras was studying the image on the screen. 'Probably about twelve or thirteen weeks, I would say. So we're talking about an expected date of confinement at the end of October.'

'I'm not going through with it! It's my body and —'

'It's Geoffrey's baby as well,' Adonis Patras interrupted, his voice gentle but firm. 'Don't you think we ought to bring in the father and see what he thinks of the situation?'

The patient glanced at the screen for the first time before covering her face with her hands. 'It's moving. . .it's alive.'

'Of course the baby's moving,' Pippa said gently. 'You've got a healthy baby inside you growing all the time — living proof of your love for Geoffrey.'

As she said this her eyes met the doctor's and she wondered if he would think her innate romanticism had gone too far. Perhaps she should be more clinical. But she needn't have feared, because he was nodding in approval.

'This will be the most rewarding event of your life, Gina,' he said. 'If you only knew how many patients I've seen who long to have babies and can't.'

He paused as he put out his hand towards the

patient. Gina hesitated for a moment before grasping it and looking up into the charismatic doctor's eyes.

'I'd like to bring Geoffrey in at this point,' Dr Patras said quietly. 'He's only just along the corridor in the medical unit. He's been asking to come and see you, but we left instructions that you weren't to be disturbed. I think you're strong enough to see him, so shall I ask Sister Manson to bring him along?'

Gina hesitated, running a hand through her short blonde hair in a distracted movement. 'If Geoffrey comes along that will mean there's no alternative. We'll have to have it then. He adores children.'

Pippa hesitated. 'But I thought you said Geoffrey wouldn't want to be tied down.'

Gina looked decidedly uncomfortable. 'Well, actually I suppose I was the one who didn't want to be tied down. I've seen what it can do to you — early marriage and all that. My sister's only twenty-five, but she looks a hundred; four children under five. I wanted Geoffrey and me to be different. I wanted us to have done something with our lives before we got married and started a family.'

'Well, life doesn't always turn out the way we plan, so we have to make the best of things,' Pippa said gently. 'Wouldn't you like me to bring Geoffrey into the discussion?'

Gina hesitated for a few moments before nodding her head. 'OK,' she said finally, in a reluctant voice. 'But don't leave me alone wth him, please. I need a bit of moral support.'

'You'll get all the support you need,' Dr Patras said firmly. 'We'll take you back to your room now and

Sister Manson will bring Geoffrey along there in a few minutes.'

Jean Granby, the red-haired Australian sister of the medical unit, was busy when Pippa arrived, but she looked up from the cardiac patient she was in the process of admitting and smiled.

'Sure; take Geoffrey along to see his girlfriend. He's been champing at the bit and he's perfectly fit now. No need to keep him in overnight. He tells me he's staying in one of the rooms down by the harbour, near the Trawler taverna. He could go back there as soon as Dr Patras has seen him again. Far better than kicking his heels around here.'

Geoffrey was silent as he walked along beside Pippa. She could sense that he was nervous of seeing his girlfriend again.

'It was a good thing you managed to hold Gina above the water this morning,' Pippa said in a quiet, sympathetic voice.

'If I hadn't known Gina as well as I do, I would have thought she was trying to drown herself,' Geoffrey replied tonelessly.

Pippa stopped in the middle of the corridor and put her hand on the young man's arm. She noticed the sad, haunted look in his eyes. His mid-brown hair was still tousled and spiky from the salt water. Obviously he hadn't taken a shower yet. He had probably been waiting in a chair, as she'd seen him when she'd done her hospital round before lunch, hoping to be called to his girlfriend's bedside.

'Why do you say that, Geoffrey?' she asked gently.

The young man shrugged. 'Because she went off into the water without telling me. I was reading in the shade of a tree and when I looked up I could see Gina out in the middle of the bay, swimming away from me. She's always been petrified of being out of her depth, and she'd been acting a bit strange recently. I just jumped up and swam out towards her. . .and then she went under.'

Pippa took a deep breath. 'But you saved her. Let's go and see her. She's waiting for you now.'

The young man's face brightened. 'I was beginning to think there was some reason why she didn't want to see me.'

Gina was sitting up in bed, wearing a crisp white hospital-issue nightdress, her blonde hair freshly combed. Adonis was standing beside the bed. He looked across towards Pippa as she walked in the room, his eyes questioning whether she had told Geoffrey anything, but she gave an almost imperceptible shake of her head.

'Come and sit down, Geoffrey,' Adonis Patras said, pulling a chair up to the side of the bed.

The young man almost collapsed on the chair, both hands reaching forward to grasp his girlfriend's.

'Are you all right, Gina? I've been so worried; I —'

'Hush, Geoffrey. . . I've got something to tell you. . . I. . .'

The patient looked up appealingly at Adonis.

'What shall I say, Doctor?'

'Tell Geoffrey the truth,' Adonis Patras replied quietly.

The patient took a deep breath and began her sad little story. Pippa noticed that, as Gina came to the part about wanting to kill herself and the unborn foetus, tears sprang into the young man's eyes. There was no anger there, only pity.

'But we can see this through together,' Geoffrey said when his girlfriend had finished speaking. 'It won't be easy, but we'll make out. And I'm dead chuffed about being a dad,' he added, with a brave attempt at a smile.

'Over five months to go yet,' the doctor put in quietly. 'And Gina's going to need all your support.'

'Of course she is. We'll get married,' Geoffrey said.

Gina pulled her hands away from Geoffrey. 'No! I don't want to get married. . .not yet. I mean, what difference does a piece of gold round your finger make?'

'It shows that you're fully committed to each other . . .and to staying together for the rest of your lives,' Pippa observed quietly.

Unwittingly her tone had become sentimental, and she sensed that Adonis Patras had picked this up and didn't approve.

'I think it's time we left these two young people together to sort out their future,' he said brusquely, moving towards the door. 'Sister and I will be near at hand. If you need us just press that bell and one of the nurses will give us a message.'

They went out into the corridor, leaving Gina and Geoffrey engrossed in their plans.

'I have a feeling it's going to be OK,' Pippa said. 'I think they'll stay together, wedding or no wedding. Gina's quite right. A wedding-ring isn't the answer. It's the true commitment that matters. Without that there's no point in continuing a relationship.'

'You sound very worldly-wise, Sister, for someone who hasn't yet made a true commitment.'

'I'm committed to my nursing career, Doctor,' she replied evenly.

He gave her a sardonic smile. 'And no one has come along to tempt you away from it?'

'If or when I make a full commitment to someone he'll have to take the career too.'

His eyes flickered momentarily. 'You're very tough for a woman.'

'Perhaps you don't know much about women. They're described as the weaker sex, but this isn't true.'

'We shall see,' he said evenly, glancing down at her foot. 'You'd better go along and settle into your room, check out your uniform and so forth, before you go over to see Dr Demetrius. I phoned him just now to say you would arrive this evening. Thank you for your help with Gina. You can start work at eight tomorrow morning. The nurse on duty at Reception will give you the key to your room. But I'd like Dr Demetrius to consider your present state of health and see what he thinks.'

Pippa bit back the retort that in her present state of health all she wanted was a warm shower before putting her feet up. But as Adonis Patras had put his word in first to Dr Demetrius she would have to force herself to keep going a bit longer.

'I'll ask Dominic Varios to take you over this evening,' Dr Patras continued before moving away, striding purposefully along the corridor.

She hesitated as she watched him go, remembering his deep brown, enigmatic eyes as he'd studied her face just now. When he let down his guard he could be very warm. And when he looked at her with that warm, fluid expression she felt something akin to excitement stirring inside her. Adonis Patras was going to be a challenge. She wanted so much to break down his initial aversion to her so that they could work easily together. And maybe, just maybe, when they got to know each other better she might find her initial assessment was wrong. She found herself hoping so.

CHAPTER THREE

THE residential medical quarters lay across a quiet courtyard. The young Greek nurse who had been sent by Reception to show Pippa to her room opened up a thick oak door and stepped back.

'Will that be all, Sister?' she asked shyly.

Pippa smiled. 'Yes, thank you, Nurse.'

The room seemed dark after the bright afternoon sunlight. Pippa flung open the wooden shutters of the window, which looked out over the courtyard. She fingered the pretty flowered chintz curtains, noticing that they were made from the same material as the bedspread over the narrow bed under the window. There was a small dressing-table, a chest of drawers, a desk against the wall by the door and an armchair. A rush mat covered part of the stone floor. It had the appearance of being a very sympathetic conversion of an old Ceres building which had obviously been here long before the hospital was built.

She sank down on the narrow bed and slipped off the big sandal that covered her injured foot. Ah, that was better! She was relieved to see a phone on the bedside table. She knew there would be times when its shrilling sound would drag her unwillingly from a deep sleep, but right now it was a godsend. She'd promised to phone home and there simply hadn't been time before.

The girl on the switchboard spoke excellent English. Pippa said she wanted to make a personal call and she would like to be billed separately from her professional calls. Better to establish that she was totally honest right from the start. It was second nature to her now to do this after the stringent policy at Benington General.

'My instructions are to permit all outward calls from senior staff, Sister Manson. You are our guest as well as our administrative sister.'

'That's very generous. Thank you.' Pippa proceeded to give the family number. She could hear the phone ringing at the other end and imagined her mother wiping her hands on a tea-towel in the warm farm kitchen. They would be two hours behind in England, but her mother would no doubt be baking.

'Pippa! What a relief to hear your voice. I've been so worried about you.'

'No need to worry, Mum. Everything's fine. The hospital is just what Nicole said it would be. . .warm and friendly — '

'How's your bad foot?'

'Splendid! Forgotten all about it.' She didn't want to add to her mother's worries!

'That's good. I thought the journey might have tired you.'

'Oh, no. I'm feeling fine. Going over to see Nicole's father-in-law tonight.'

'Oh, that'll be nice. It's a relief to know you have some family out there. Simon and Peter were here at the weekend. Simon brought his new girlfriend. Who knows? I might get one of you married and settled down before too long.'

'Who knows?' Pippa repeated. 'Got to go now, Mum. I'll keep in touch.'

'Yes; mind you do, Pippa, and do take care of yourself.'

Pippa smiled as she put down the phone. Her mother never missed a chance to point out that she wished her children would marry and settle down. Simon, a computer programmer in Manchester, was thirty-one, which her mother thought was outrageously old to be still a bachelor, and Peter, two years younger was a teacher who changed his girlfriends frequently. Pippa had often pointed out that at twenty-five she had plenty of time to think about settling down, but her mother had insisted that when she was her age she'd been a mother of three and until you'd experienced motherhood you hadn't begun to live.

Well, she was enjoying her career and intended to keep it that way for a long time.

She shuffled off the bed and moved across the room. Opening up the narrow wardrobe, she found a pale blue uniform dress and white apron. On the top shelf was a small white Sister-Dora-type cap. She tried it on in front of the mirror and grimaced at her reflection. It perched on the top of her thick dark hair like a pea on a drum! She would have to do something to tame her wild locks before she ventured back into the hospital. A shampoo and lots of conditioner were called for, and maybe. . .just maybe she would have a couple of inches taken off her hair. Or she could wind it up on top.

The problem of her hair absorbed her as she moved through the curtained alcove. What bliss! Her own tiny shower-room. No corridors to negotiate when she was dead on her feet. And to think, she'd had to come all the way from London to a remote Greek island to achieve such luxury.

Easing off the crêpe bandage, she examined her foot. The swelling was going down. It would be good to bathe it.

The water was hot as it cascaded over her body. She stood with her face upturned as she rubbed the shampoo into her hair. Mmm, that felt good! Now the conditioner. She could feel the silky smoothness as she ran her fingers through her hair. She wanted to look good when she next went on duty.

Was that someone knocking on the door? She frowned as she reached forward and turned off the shower. Wrapped in a large fluffy towel, she went back into her room. The knock came again. She realised she didn't have anything to put on except the travel-stained skirt and shirt. Presumably her suitcase was still on board the Capodistrias boat.

'Who is it?' she called tentatively.

'Ariadne Stangos. I've come to see if there's anything you need.'

'Oh, Sister Stangos; thank goodness it's you and not . . .not anyone else,' she finished off hastily. Pulling the large towel around her sarong-style, she opened up the door.

Sister Stangos was smiling as she stepped into the room. 'I knew nobody would have thought about your mufti clothes. They're still on the boat, aren't they?' She sank down into the armchair and tossed a plastic bag on to the bed. 'I've brought you my spare dressing-gown, a clean shirt and underwear. You're thinner than me, but it's better than nothing. You'll be able to settle yourself in when you get your case back. You're going to Symborio this evening, aren't you? Dominic asked me to say that he'll be ready to take you over there about six. I understand Dr Demetrius wants to see you before you officially start work.'

'Yes, that's right. And I've promised Nicole to keep an eye on her father-in-law while I'm here. I suppose a weekly visit will be enough. To be honest, I wish I didn't have to go this evening. It's been quite a day!'

'Yes, how's your foot? Sudek's atrophy can cause problems. Are you sure you should be working so soon?'

'Don't you start!' Pippa said wryly. 'I've got to convince Dr Patras that I'm OK for duty. I know I'm doing the right thing. The more I can use the foot, the stronger it will become. The only danger is knocking it while it's still in a weakened state.'

'As you did this morning,' Sister Stangos put in sympathetically,

'Exactly! That was the problem I was dreading. Anyway, things can only get better. Thank you so much for bringing me these clothes,' Pippa said, disappearing into her shower-room for a few seconds before emerging in the large cotton dressing-gown.

Ariadne's plump face creased up as she laughed. 'It's a bit like a bell tent on you. I expect you have something much prettier in your suitcase. You can change on the way over to Symborio.'

'Tell me about Nicole's father-in-law,' Pippa said, a note of apprehension slipping into her voice.

'Well, I've always found that Dr Demetrius Capodistrias, who, as you probably know, is the founder and benefactor of this hospital, insists on keeping his finger on the pulse. He's a dear old boy really, but he can be a bit overpowering, so make sure you don't commit yourself to too many visits over there.'

Pippa sat on the bed, her injured foot stretched out

in front of her, while she fixed the crêpe bandage. She looked across at the kindly Greek sister. 'I'd much rather stay here all the time, but I suppose I'll have to conform, for Nicole's sake.'

'You'll be interested to hear that the Capodistrias house is very near to the Patras residence. The two families see a lot of each other. . .dinner parties and so on,' Sister Stangos finished off, her eyes fixed on Pippa.

Pippa gave her colleague a glazed smile. 'And why should that interest me?'

Ariadne laughed. 'Oh, come on, Pippa. . .may I call you Pippa?'

'Of course, but——'

'I know you found Adonis Patras very daunting when you first arrived, but I expect you sensed that if you could break through his antagonism he'd be a most attractive man. So if you get to know him socially—out there at Symborio for instance—then you might find——'

'Honestly, Ariadne, you're way off the mark! The man is far too arrogant and conceited for my liking. I've no desire to form any kind of relationship with him other than a professional one.'

Ariadne smiled. 'That's because you don't know him yet. He can drive women wild. Most of the staff here were so excited when we heard he was coming to work for six months. He only has to crook his little finger and——'

'He'd better not crook his little finger at me. I have no desire to fall all over him,' Pippa replied in a dry tone.

'Well, that's just as well, because he's spoken for.'

'I suppose you mean Cassiopi Manoulis?'

'Yes, have you met her.'

'She came along the harbourside when we were having lunch. She seems very charming.'

'No need to be charitable. She's a very dangerous woman and she'll scratch your eyes out if she thnks you're going to try and take her man from her.

'Nothing could be further from my mind.'

'Well, I'm glad about that, because it wouldn't do you any good. The families wouldn't allow anything to break up the expected marriage.'

'And when will that be?'

'Oh, maybe this year, maybe next. They keep putting it off for one reason or another. Cassiopi went to America for several years to stay with another branch of the family and Adonis was busy in Athens. I've always thought it was a marriage of convenience made by the two families. It's not a conventional love-match, more a merger of two rich dynasties who recognise that they can prosper financially by the marriage.'

'But Dr Patras must have some feeling for this woman, hasn't he? I mean he doesn't strike me as being the sort of man who would be pushed into a liaison against his wishes.'

'I think Adonis finds it convenient to go along with. He's essentially a career man, as far as I can gather. . . Well, I mean he's a very important medical professor in Athens. About five years ago, when the Capodistrias and Patras families were over for their summer vacation at their houses in Symborio Bay, we were all invited to the betrothal party of Cassiopi and Adonis. Cassiopi looked radiant, as well she might after two disastrous marriages ending in divorce. To suddenly become the bride-to-be again was like a shot in the arm. . . Oh, dear, am I sounding too catty?'

Pippa gave a wry smile. 'You're making it obvious you don't like her. I must admit I didn't exactly take to her myself. But tell me, how did Dr Patras look at this betrothal party? Presumably he must have given his consent.'

Ariadne frowned. 'That was the strange part about it. I've known Adonis since he was a boy. He was born here in the Patras summer residence and he used to come back here from Athens every summer. I'm thirty-seven — the same age as Cassiopi, although she looks years younger, probably due to that expensive face-lift she had. . . Oh, dear, here I go again! Anyway, Adonis is a couple of years older and he was always a heart-throb to the girls. And Cassiopi used to chase him — oh, so much. But he went away to London to medical school and. . .heavens! Is that the time? I'll have to go. I only popped out for a few minutes and my staff nurse will never be able to cope with the evening feeds and baths.'

'Let me give you a hand to make up for lost time,' Pippa said, warming to her new colleague. 'It won't take me a minute to throw on my uniform, and I've got a couple of hours before the boat leaves for Symborio.'

'But you're off duty. . .'

'Now look here, Sister Stangos, who's in charge here?' Pippa interrupted, with a wry grin.

Ariadne laughed. 'So sorry, ma'am. Here, give me your apron and I'll fix the buttons.'

The cries from the obstetrics and nursery unit could be heard all down the corridor. Pippa smiled as they pushed open the door and went in among the cots.

'It sounds like sheep-shearing time on the fells back home where I come from.'

A harassed-looking staff nurse was rushing in from the small feeds preparation kitchen, a feeding bottle in each hand. Pippa took hold of one of the bottles.

'Who's this for, Staff Nurse?'

The staff nurse pointed to a baby in the cot at the far corner of the unit. 'That's for Nico. He's a four-week-old prem and he needs every drop, Sister.'

Pippa took the bottle to the bedside and looked down at the small, dark baby lying on his back, whimpering gently to attract attention. She put the bottle down on the table beside the cot and picked up the little mite.

'Poor little Nico,' she crooned against the warm face.

The wailing stopped and the baby snuggled against her, his little lips searching against the white apron in the hope of appeasing his thirst.

'Just a moment, darling; let me get settled on this chair and then. . .' She checked the temperature of the bottle on the back of her hand before putting the teat gently into the baby's mouth. She smiled down at the dark, fluffy hair on top of Nico's head. He was so content now.

'Where's the baby's mother, Sister?' she asked Ariadne, who was feeding the baby in the next cot.

'She's at home, looking after her other four children. The eldest is sixteen and the next three range in age down to nine. Little Nico wasn't exactly planned, particularly his birth. He came five weeks early, which was a shock to all the family and ——'

Ariadne stopped in mid-sentence as the door opened

and Adonis Patras walked in. He moved across the room swiftly to stand between Ariadne and Pippa.

'I thought I explained you weren't on duty until tomorrow, Sister Manson. Your devotion to duty is admirable. . .or was it merely an opportunity to have a gossip? Sister Stangos holds the world record for gossip. Ask her anything you want to know about the people on this island and she will be able to tell you. If she doesn't know it, she will readily find out. In fact we don't need a newspaper on Ceres. Sister Stangos is our reliable source of information.'

Pippa looked up into the dark, enigmatic eyes and frowned. 'Sister Stangos has been most helpful since I arrived. I'm not sure that I approve of your tone, Dr Patras.'

She was aware that Ariadne was looking uncomfortable, but she felt she had to defend her colleague.

The doctor placed one hand on the back of Pippa's chair and looked down at her. She could feel his hot breath fanning her face and there was an aroma of aftershave that disturbed her. Ariadne had told her that Adonis had been a heart-throb in his youth. He hadn't changed. He still thought he only had to look at a girl to set her pulses racing.

'Don't worry about Ariadne,' he said in a quiet voice. 'We go back a long way, and she knows how I feel about the tales that are spread around. You mustn't believe everything you're told.'

He pulled himself to his full height and looked around the room. 'Don't get up, ladies. I can see you've got your hands full, so I'll just do a round by myself.'

Pippa watched as Adonis moved from cot to cot, examining each baby before checking all the infor-

mation on their charts. It was obvious that he loved
his work and adored babies. She placed the empty
feeding bottle on the side-table and held baby Nico
against her as she gently patted his back. 'Come along,
Nico. Let's have a little burp,' she whispered to the
tiny mite, who was snuggling against her, eyes closed,
threatening to fall asleep with the wind still inside him.

Out of the corner of her eye she could see the doctor
cradling one of the babies in his arms, and found
herself wondering how he could agree to a loveless
marriage. He didn't appear spineless or easily persuaded. So what kind of hold did Cassiopi have over
him. . .? Or maybe it was the families who were
exerting their weight.

She dropped her eyes as he suddenly looked across,
and gave her full attention to the baby.

'Ah, there's a good boy,' she murmured as she
heard and felt the awaited burp. 'Now I can change
your nappy and put you down in your cot.'

All through the nappy-changing operation she could
feel Adonis's eyes on her. He was sitting at the desk,
writing up medication, but between each chart that
Ariadne Stangos handed to him he glanced across. It
made her nervous. Was he sizing her up, seeing if she
was up to the job? Certainly she felt confident when
she was sitting down, but it was when she had to move
around that the problems started. She settled little
Nico on his back; the little eyes fluttered open briefly
before he fell asleep.

The door opened again and Dominic Varios, the
young Greek doctor, came in.

'I'm looking for Sister Manson. . .ah, there you are,
Sister. I was told you'd gone to your room. We have to

leave earlier than planned. Dr Demetrius Capodistrias
has just telephoned. I didn't know you were working.'

'Devotion to duty, Dr Varios,' Adonis observed
drily. 'But if Dr Demetrius has sent a summons you'd
better go.'

Dominic was looking impatient. 'How soon can you
be ready, Sister? Dr Demetrius said——'

'You go ahead,' Adonis intervened. 'I'd like Sister
Manson to see one of the patients with me. . . Gina,
the girl who nearly drowned this morning. She's just
next door. I'll bring Sister over in about half an hour.
Go and keep the peace with the old man and prepare
the welcome party.'

Pippa opened her mouth to remonstrate, but
thought better of it. She didn't relish another confrontation with the high-handed doctor. And her professional interest in their new patient swayed her to go
along with his plans. She would be happy to have a
chance to talk to Gina again and find out what her
difficult patient had decided.

Neither of them spoke as they walked the short way
between the different units to the gynaecological
department.

Gina's boyfriend, Geoffrey, was sitting on the bed
when Pippa and Adonis went in, and Pippa divined,
from the radiant look on Geoffrey's face, that he'd
talked Gina round to his way of thinking.

'We'd like to get married out here,' Geoffrey said
when they'd broken the good news. 'There's no point
going back and upsetting our parents. And I've got no
job in England. I'll try and find work on the island. . .
Anything would do.'

'We need another porter,' Adonis Patras said.

Geoffrey smiled. 'Fantastic! When can I start?'

'As soon as you can give me a reference. I'd like the name of someone you've worked for, so that I can phone him up. You did have a job, I take it?'

Geoffrey nodded. 'I did work experience when I was at school and then I got a job in a garage; I was made redundant after a year, but the boss said he would give me a good reference.'

'Well, that should be OK, then. Meanwhile we'd better keep Gina in for a few days' observation before she joins you again. You've got a room down by the Trawler taverna, I hear.'

'Yes. It's fairly basic, but very clean. . .and extremely cheap, which is the main thing at the moment. I'll try and get something better for when the baby's born.'

Pippa and Dr Patras left the happy couple in the care of one of the staff nurses and went out into the corridor.

'You'd better go and change out of your uniform, Sister,' he told her briskly. 'Meet me in Reception when you're ready.'

Pippa felt decidedly unfashionable in Ariadne's capacious cotton shirt and her own travel-stained skirt as she walked into Reception. Adonis was waiting for her by the door, tapping his foot impatiently.

'What interesting clothes! Dr Capodistrias will be charmed to met you,' he said as he led her out through the main door.

'I've got some clothes in my suitcase. . . Oh, drat! The suitcase is in Dominic's boat. I could have ——'

'No, it's not. I've arranged for it to be put on mine. So you can change on the way over.'

'You've thought of everything, haven't you?'

When they reached the harbour Pippa could see a tall Greek sailor standing by one of the larger speed boats. He saw Pippa and held out his hand to help her on board. Almost immediately the boat left the quayside, weaving in and out of the boats tied up in the harbour.

The fresh air hit her and she breathed in. Adonis was standing beside her as they left the bright lights of Ceres Town and headed off across the darkening water. The sun was slowly sinking into the sea beyond the horizon, painting orange streaks across the midnight-blue of the waer.

'Go below and change, Sister. You'd better put on something that will gladden the old man's heart,' Dr Patras instructed.

Clinging to the iron rails of the ladder, she reached the cabin and leaned against the door to recover from the exertion. She'd left her stick on deck, so she had to hobble around the narrow cabin, holding on to the bunks. Her suitcase was on the bottom bunk. She opened it up and rummaged around, deciding that the green silk shirt which she'd so carefully wrapped in tissue paper would be ideal for the occasion. So many of her friends had told her it went well with her dark hair and brought out the green in her eyes. And she would wear the white linen skirt with the Italian leather belt from the January sales in Harrods, but her feet wouldn't fit into the matching leather sandals. She laid the items out on the bunk so that she could slip into them easily. As she peeled off the functional but unflattering shirt she convinced herself that this rich old ex-shipping magnate turned philanthropic doctor would be sure to approve of her outfit tonight.

And Nicole would be proud to hear that her cousin

was a credit to the family, which was the object of the exercise.

Carefully she hauled herself back up on deck and sat down on the bench seat opposite Adonis. She looked across and was surprised to see the undisguised admiration in his eyes. But then he was a man, wasn't he? He noticed when a girl had made an improvement to her appearance. And any change from her previous outfit had got to be for the better!

He raised his eyes to the sky. 'See how the sun has almost set.'

She looked out at the huge glow and leaned towards the gentle waves. The crimson fingers of the sunset were shining on the brass railing that ran the length of the boat. And out on the water the iridescent flecks of foam danced against the scenic backcloth of the approaching mountainside.

The boat skimmed through the water and pulled in to a wooden jetty.

'That's the Capodistrias residence,' Adonis Patras said, pointing upwards to a white crenellated building overlooking the sea. 'And higher, to the right, is the Patras family home.'

Pippa could see the bare outline of another white building, also crenellated in the manner of a castle.

'Impressive!' she breathed. 'I was told that Cassiopi's family have a house in the bay too.'

'Yes, we're all here. Three dynasties fighting for survival. On the surface all is peaceful and prosperous, but underneath. . .' He spread his hands and shrugged his shoulders. 'Who can tell what the future holds?'

'And the Manoulis house?'

'It's up there. . .at the top of the mountain.'

Pippa strained her eyes to see Cassiopi's house in

the gathering gloom. The sun had disappeared and the mountain was black. At the top of it she could just make out a long white building that was definitely a castle. Whereas the Patras and the Capodistrias houses had the appearance of castles, this was in no doubt about its superior status.

'It's centuries old and dates back to the time when the islanders had to defend themselves against marauding pirates. The Manoulis family bought it at the turn of the century, restored it, and made it into a luxury residence.'

'They must be very rich. Where does all the money come from?'

Adonis's eyes flickered ominously. 'Who knows? They have a great many businesses both in Greece and other parts of the world. When you're as rich as the Manoulis family no one asks questions.'

The boat was being tied up. A sailor held out both hands to help Pippa across the gangplank.

She looked back towards the cabin. 'My suitcase?'

'It will be taken to the Capodistrias house, madam,' the sailor told her. 'Come this way. Dr Demetrius is expecting you.' He glanced at Dr Patras. 'Dr Demetrius asked me to extend an invitation to dinner tonight, Dr Patras.'

Pippa didn't know why she held her breath as she waited for the answer.

'Please give my regards to Dr Demetrius and say that I have a previous engagement.' His eyes rested briefly on Pippa's upturned, expectant face, and she turned away, annoyed at the wild beating of her heart.

CHAPTER FOUR

PIPPA wasn't prepared for the frail appearance of Dr Demetrius Capodistrias. The old, white-haired medical philanthropist was sitting in a deep armchair beside a wide stone fireplace. Although the evening was cool, it seemed to Pippa that it didn't warrant the fire that flickered against the antique black iron fireback.

'I'm always cold,' Dr Demetrius said, by way of explanation. 'When you're over eighty your poor old bones need warming up. But I'm concerned about you. Nicole told me about your unfortunate accident with the broken glass and the subsequent operation. And Dominic informs me you hurt the foot again today, which is why you're having to use that stick. Now, my dear, tell me honestly, do you think you're going to be able to cope with your new job?'

'Of course I am! My foot is getting stronger all the time. I just have to be careful not to walk over uneven surfaces for a while, and you must admit the Ceres harbourside is like an assault course.' She was smiling at the old man to reassure him and forestall him making an unfavourable opinion about her.

Dr Demetrius gave a sigh of resignation. 'Well, come and sit beside me, my dear, and tell me what you think of my hospital.'

Pippa explained that she'd spent only a few hours there but she was decidedly impressed with the place.

'It was necessary that I have it built,' the old man said. 'As a young man I was only interested in making

63

money. But later I felt I should do something for the people of my birthplace, so I built the hospital and studied medicine in Athens before working here. Then my dear son Alexander followed in my footsteps. As you know, he and Nicole now have two sons and a daughter, and I hope one or two of the children will become doctors.'

The supper was served in the oak-panelled dining-room at a long, ornate, highly polished wooden table, laden with silver cutlery that gleamed in the light of the heavy antique candelabra. There was only one other person at the table besides Pippa and Dr Demetrius. Dominic Varios was an entertaining young man and obviously doted on by the older doctor, who had known him since he was a child and treated him like a son. Eirene, Dominic's mother, served the supper and smiled proudly at the son who had risen from being a child of the servants to a professional man respected by all the islanders.

Pippa enjoyed the rack of lamb and a delicious pudding made from honey, but she ate sparingly. She rarely ate both lunch and supper, and today was an exception which she found difficult to cope with.

'You're tired, my dear,' Dr Demetrius observed as she failed to stifle a yawn when they were drinking their coffee on the veranda overlooking the sea. 'Please feel free to go up to bed. You've had a very long day. Dominic will keep me company until Adonis arrives.'

'Dr Patras is coming here?'

'He telephoned to thank me for my invitation to dinner and explained that he is spending the evening with the Manoulis family but that he would come along after dinner.'

She stood up, fighting down the desire to stay up. Her feelings were muddled. Firstly, she wanted to make sure that Adonis Patras wasn't going to persuade Dr Demetrius that her appointent had been unwise. And secondly. . .she couldn't understand why she simply wanted to see the impossible man again in an off-duty situation.

'Goodnight,' she said quietly.

Dominic rose to his feet. 'I will be ready to take you over to the hospital at seven, Sister.'

'Thank you, Dominic.'

'I shall still be in bed when you leave, my dear,' the old doctor said. 'So I won't see you until you come again. Make it soon. I've enjoyed your company this evening. Come over whenever your hospital duties permit.'

Pippa promised she would. At last she was beginning to feel secure in her new appointment!

The guest room she was to sleep in overlooked the bay. She had already been up there before supper to wash her hands and tidy her hair, but now she was able to give it a more thorough scrutiny. She liked what she saw. A thick cream woollen carpet covered the middle of the floor. The wood block surrounds were polished to a high sheen. The double bed, with its handmade white Grecian counterpane, felt firm and comfortable as she sat down upon it. The pillows were soft and feathery, simply asking to be sunk into.

She lay back and looked up at the white alabaster ceiling, admiring the vine-leaf motif that edged the central cluster of cherubic angels. She smiled to herself as she thought that, although she wasn't used to such unashamed luxury, she could easily become accustomed to it.

She tensed as she heard voices below in the hall: the deep sound of Adonis Patras's laughter, mingling with the tinkling chatter of Cassiopi. It seemed that their relationship was more than one of convenience, and she surprised herself by feeling disappointed. Maybe Ariadne was right when she'd pointed out that sooner or later she would get romantic ideas about Adonis Patras. But she would certainly fight against such notions! The man had been impossibly rude to her when she'd arrived and she wasn't going to waste any emotion on someone who could be so high-handed and unfeeling on an occasion which should have been welcoming. No, her initial opinion had been right. He'd shown himself in his true colours.

She was waiting at the quayside at seven. Eirene had wakened her at about six with a tray of coffee, rolls, honey and fresh peaches. There was far more breakfast than she required, but she made an effort to eat something to give her strength for the unknown day ahead.

The strong Greek coffee had set her mind buzzing and, with her first waking thoughts, she'd remembered Adonis Patras, that maddeningly charismatic Greek doctor who'd tried to put her in her place. . .indeed, had tried to send her packing in the first instance. She would be working with him today and she was going to show him what she was made of!

Carefully she had removed the crêpe bandage and found, to her relief, that the swelling had gone down. She would put some weight on the foot today and dispense with the stick. Yesterday's setback had only been temporary. And, as her orthopaedic consultant at the Benington had told her, if she could walk through the pain she would strengthen the foot.

She had smiled at herself in the mirror. That was the first step: look cheerful; look normal; don't let anyone guess that there's anything wrong with you. Easier said than done, but it was the only way out of her dilemma. She'd committed herself to this job, and no one — and especially not the obnoxious Dr Patras — was going to accuse her of ducking out of her medical duties.

She walked slowly down to the water's edge, her steps gathering momentum as she found her feet. She looked out over the sea in the early morning sunlight and wondered what strategies she should employ when working side by side with Adonis Patras. She decided she would have to be totally detached from all emotion, to think only of her patients, and to be completely professional. And she must appear to be physically and mentally strong so that he couldn't criticise her work. It wasn't going to be easy, but nothing worth while ever was.

She remembered now the sound of laughter last night from downstairs. It was quite a party that she'd missed! If only she'd stayed up she might have found out more about the mysterious relationship between Adonis Patras and Cassiopi Manoulis. But from what she'd heard it sounded as if the relationship was genuine, as if they intended to get married. And what could be more suitable? They were a couple who were both from rich, aristocratic Greek families, raised together since childhood, with business interests that concerned both families. Their compatibility list was endless.

She bent down and dipped her hand into the water

of the bay. It felt cool, yet deliciously inviting. An early morning swim would have been a good idea if only she'd had the time.

Even as the thought occurred to her she heard the sound of someone calling her name.

'Sister Manson!'

It was Adonis Patras, standing dripping water on to the deck of his boat as it rounded the headland. He was wearing a pair of black, sleekly fitting swimming-trunks that looked as if they'd been sprayed on to his body.

She took a deep breath as he leapt ashore and came running along the wooden jetty towards her.

'Have you been swimming, Sister?'

She moved backwards, almost defensively, brushing a hand over her uniform dress as if to remind herself of her intended professionalism.

'I haven't had time. Dominic wants to leave at seven and —'

'Swimming is good for your injured foot. It's the best exercise you can have, because you can exercise the muscles without any weight bearing.' Adonis Patras's face was wreathed in smiles as he ran a hand through his wet dark hair. 'But perhaps you're not feeling up to it. In that case —'

'I'm fine! Look, no stick today.' She hated herself for being so anxious to please this exacting man.

'Then you simply must have a swim before you go on duty. All work and no play. . . I can't remember the rest of your English proverb, but you know what I mean. Go back to the house and take your uniform off and put on a swimsuit. I'll wait here. Dominic hasn't got his boat ready yet. I'll take you over on mine.'

She hesitated, knowing that she would have no

problem in the water, but it was climbing in and out that would be difficult. She glanced at the rocks sheering into the sea. It would be deep enough to dive, and she'd think about getting out later. Yes, a swim was just what she needed to prepare for the day ahead.

She walked back to the house, aware that the doctor was watching her. She was moving as quickly as she dared without making any mistakes this time. Her suitcase was still beside the kitchen door, where Eirene had placed it for Dominic to take down to his boat. She rummaged around, took out her white bikini, and went back to the guest room where she'd spent the night.

Adonis Patras was swimming around near the quayside when she got back. Slipping off the towel that she'd wrapped around her, she dived into the sea.

Down, down, down she went, and shivered as she saw the sheer depth of the water. It was like looking at an upturned mountain! And so clear. She could see the multicoloured fish swimming alongside as she began to surface.

Adonis Patras swam towards her as she surfaced, his rugged frame too near for comfort.

'Where did you learn to swim like that?' he asked, treading water.

'There's a tarn. . .that's a small lake. . .on our farm in the Lake District in the north of England. My parents taught my brothers and me to swim when we were very small, so that they wouldn't have to worry about us falling in. In fact I can't remember when I couldn't swim. It comes as easily as walking. And the water of the tarn is so cold that any other lake or sea is always warm by comparison.'

'You talk of brothers. How many do you have?'

'I've got two brothers—both older. . . Look, this is a strange place to hold a conversation.' For one second she had glanced down at the sheer drop beneath her. 'I know I said that I was as happy swimming as walking, but that doesn't mean I'm immune to vertigo. This bay makes our little tarn seem like a shallow pond.'

'OK, let's swim back to the jetty. It's time we were getting back to our patients.'

They swam back towards the rocky shore and once Pippa felt her arm brush against the doctor's. It sent a *frisson* of conflicting sensation running down her spine. Here in the water it was so easy to forgot that this was a man who had opposed her appointment and didn't want her to succeed in her job.

He had reached the jetty before her and she circled around uncertainly, wondering which tack to take. She didn't want him to see how the problem of getting out of the water was worrying her. Suddenly he turned and held both hands out towards her.

'Let me help you, Philippa.'

Her mind registered with surprise his familiar use of her name. 'Thanks, but I can manage.'

'There's no need to be so independent. It's only what I would do to help any girl out of the water. There's such a thing as old-fashioned courtesy.'

She was sure he was mocking her, but it was easier to comply than swim around in the water arguing.

His fingers when they clasped around hers were firm and the grip was sensuously exciting. But, looking up into his eyes as he hauled her out, she was sure she saw an expression of triumph.

She had to accept Adonis Patras's offer of a ride in his boat, because Dominic had left some time before.

But she made sure that it took only minutes for her to go back to the house and change into her uniform.

Night Sister was waiting to give Pippa a full report when she arrived at the hospital, so she went into the sister's office. It transpired that it had been a quiet night with no further admissions or emergencies. After the report, Pippa set off on her round of the in-patients, checking out the charts with the information that Night Sister had given her.

In the obstetrics unit she found Gina in good spirits.

'I'd like to go home today, Sister.'

Pippa raised her eyebrows. 'Home?'

Gina giggled. 'Not home to England. Mum would never forgive me. She's terribly religious and she doesn't approve of fallen women like me. No, I mean I want to go back to the little room Geoffrey and I share down by the harbour.'

'Well, hold on a bit, till Dr Patras has seen you. And Gina, I really think you ought to write to your mother and tell her you've decided to stay on. There's no need to mention the baby just yet. But she'll have to know eventually, won't she?'

'I suppose so,' Gina admitted grudgingly. 'Well, I'll send her a postcard to begin with, and then later on I'll have a think about it. Maybe after we're married I won't feel so scared of her.'

'Why don't you invite your parents out to the wedding?'

Gina shuddered. 'No fear! Look, I'll send a postcard now and then write again after we're married.'

Pippa gave her a sympathetic smile. 'Well, if that's what you think is best. I suppose you know your own parents better than I do.'

She felt for her patient's pulse. Full, strong and bounding. She glanced at the charts. Blood-pressure normal. Gina certainly seemed none the worse for her near drowning. In fact the whole episode had brought things to a head and sorted out the problem. Pippa couldn't help wondering if the suicide attempt had merely been a cry for help from a very confused young woman who couldn't make up her mind what it was she actually wanted. Well, the supposition was entirely academic. What mattered was that Gina and Geoffrey were now united in their common cause of producing a healthy baby and providing a stable environment.

Pippa promised to speak to the doctor about discharging Gina, before moving on to the nursery, where the bleating cries reminded her of the lambing season back home.

Ariadne Stangos smiled at her above the head of a tiny mite who was sucking at his bottle with eyes closed.

'Do you have time to help with the feeds, Sister Manson?' she asked. 'We're running behind schedule again. Chrisanthe, my part-time nurse, didn't turn up. . . She sent a message to say she isn't well enough to come in. I'm going to have to check her out when she comes back, because this is the second time in a week she's let me down. She seems to forget she's getting paid for her work.'

'Let me have a chat with her when she next shows up,' Pippa said. 'Meanwhile, I'd love to feed one of the babes. How about Nico?'

Pippa glanced across at the dark little prem, who was bawling his head off. 'Something tells me Nico hasn't been fed yet,' she added, as she made for the feeds kitchen.

'How clever of you! The power of professional training!' Ariadne observed drily. 'No wonder you were such a whiz-kid at your hospital when you can make such an accurate diagnosis, Sister Manson.'

'I can't think why everyone has got the idea that I'm some kind of special nurse,' Pippa said, returning from the kitchen and relaxing against her chair as Nico began to suck on the bottle, reducing the nursery noise by several welcome decibels.

'Your dear cousin Nicole was very fond of talking about you. Most of us were in awe of what you would actually be like when we heard you were coming out here. So it's a relief to find you're only human. And we certainly didn't expect you to arrive in the ambulance. How is your foot today?'

'It's been much worse in the past, but it will get better as time passes. In fact, before I leave here, I expect to be one hundred per cent fit.'

'Well, I hope everyone co-operates.'

'If you're referring to his lordship, you don't need to worry. I can handle him.'

Ariadne smiled. 'I should think you can. Whose idea was it to go swimming this morning?'

Pippa bent her head over the baby to cover up the infuriating flush that was spreading across her cheeks. 'News travels fast,' she said, in a matter-of-fact tone.

'I heard Dominic explaining to Night Sister that you would be in at eight, not seven-thirty.'

'I'm not due in until eight,' Pippa countered. 'And I felt like a swim. I used to swim every morning, winter and summer alike, when I lived at home. It didn't matter to me who I was swimming with, because it was so beautiful out there in Symborio Bay.'

She raised her eyes and saw the whimsical

expression on Ariadne's face. Her own eyes, she was sure, must be betraying the fact that yes, she had found the handsome Greek doctor exciting at close quarters. She would have to be made of stone not to feel his extraordinary charisma.

She was sure that this astute Greek woman, who was, after all, twelve years her senior, must have felt the strong magnetic attraction of the man. She wondered just how much experience of men Ariadne had, because she looked so content with life, the sort of woman who had experienced everything and decided to settle for what she'd got. She could be the sort of friend Pippa needed to confide in. . .but then again she might simply be someone who enjoyed a good gossip and passing on the latest tittle-tattle to anyone who would listen. It was difficult to decide which.

Pippa put the half-empty bottle on the side-table and held the baby against her until he burped. Then, carefully placing the teat back in his mouth, she looked across at Ariadne. The Greek sister was placing one of the babies back in his cot and crooning gently to him.

'There are so many things I need to know about this island, Ariadne,' she began. 'Tell me about the people who live here all the time. Is there any animosity between the true islanders and the rich people who come and go like —— ?'

She broke off as the door opened and Adonis Patras came striding down the nursery, his eyes wide with curiosity.

'Is this a private conversation or can anyone listen in?'

Pippa bridled. 'Sister and I are having a private conversation.'

The doctor's enigmatic eyes flickered. 'So I see. I

would prefer it if the two of you got on with your work
and left the gossip until later.'

Pippa drew in her breath. It was grossly unfair of
Adonis Patras to take that tone, but she wouldn't
labour the issue. He was quite right. Personal and
professional lives shouldn't be mixed.

She looked down at the tiny mite in her arms. His
eyes had closed. He was falling asleep before he'd
finished his feed, having exhausted himself with crying
beforehand. Gently, she tried to waken him; he slum-
bered on, so she gave up trying and settled him back
in his cot.

'I'll send you another nurse, Sister Stangos,' she said
in her most professional voice. 'The babies mustn't be
made to wait for their feeds because of staff absence.'

Adonis looked up from the charts he was studying.
'Who's missing today?'

'Nurse Chrisanthe,' Ariadne replied brusquely.
'Twice this week, without an adequate excuse, except
she didn't feel well enough to come in. If there's
somthing wrong with her we'd better get her examined; if not, then she can stop messing me about.'

'I saw her just now, coming out of the baker's down
by the harbour,' Adonis Patras said. 'I was looking out
of my window. I assumed she was having a day off.'

'She's having a day off all right! But getting paid for
working,' Ariadne said.

'I'll deal with her when she comes back,' Pippa said
quietly. 'There may be a good reason for her absence.'

'There'd better be,' Ariadne replied ominously.

'Gina was asking to see you, Dr Patras,' Pippa said
quickly. 'She wants to leave us.'

'I'll go and see her now,' he replied. 'I'd like you to

come with me. I think a full examination will be necessary before I can discharge Gina.'

Gina's eyes shone with pleasure as Pippa and the doctor arrived.

'You're going to let me go home, aren't you Doctor? I want to start getting everything ready for my baby.'

'Not so fast, Gina. I want to check you over first. Sister will get you ready, so just relax.'

He scrubbed up at the sink as Pippa prepared her patient. Gina held on to Pippa's hand as he gave her a full examination. At the end he smiled confidently.

'Everything is in its right place and your blood tests and so on are normal. So we'll let you go this morning, but I want you to check in each week so I can keep tabs on you. It's going to be difficult settling in to a new life out here and having a baby. I suppose you haven't changed your mind about staying here?'

Gina shook her head. 'I'm not going back to England. I'll tell my parents about the baby after it's born, but not before.'

The doctor gave his patient a sympathetic smile. 'Well, I must respect your wishes, but personally I think a girl needs her mother to know what's going on. You'd be surprised how a mother's attitude can change when her daughter confides that she's going to have a baby.'

'Not mine!' Gina said grimly.

'We'll arrange an appointment for you at Out-patients,' Adonis Patras said, recognising that the girl's mind was made up and there was nothing more he could do to sway her.

'Talking of which,' he continued, pausing by the door, 'it's time we started the Out-patients' clinic.

Would you spend the morning with me, Sister Manson, or do you have something more important to accomplish? Sister Arama spent a lot of time on administration in her office, so I'll understand if you haven't got time.'

'I intend to delegate as much paperwork as possible to the medical secretary,' Pippa replied quickly, touched by the courteous approach. 'I prefer nursing to pen-pushing, so I'd like to assist you this morning, Doctor. It will give me a chance to meet some of the islanders.'

She turned back to look at her patient as Adonis Patras held open the door. 'You can get dressed now, Gina. I'll send a message to Geoffrey asking him to come and collect you.'

'Thanks, Sister.'

It took Pippa only half an hour to work through the priority administration with Elena, her Greek secretary, in the bright, sunny office overlooking the harbour. Then, leaving instructions that she would be in Out-patients, she went along to join Adonis.

'Dr Patras is with an emergency patient,' the Out-patient staff nurse told her. 'He's in the first cubicle.'

Pippa pulled aside the curtains and walked in. The doctor's back was towards her, but her eyes fell immediately on the prostrate figure on the examination couch.

'Oh, no!' She clapped her hand over her mouth to stifle the gasp of horror. It couldn't be. . .but it was. Oh, of all the bad luck!

She reached forward and took hold of the patient's hand. 'I've just sent a message for you to come to the hospital to take Gina home,' she said gently to the young man. 'What happened?'

Adonis Patras turned and spoke gently to Pippa. 'Geoffrey was helping out one of the builders who was renovating a house on the hillside. He needed a job until we could employ him as a porter. Some of the scaffolding gave way and he fell. It looks like a fractured femur to me. They've only just brought him in. Get me a syringe and some pethidine stat!'

CHAPTER FIVE

THE X-rays revealed that Geoffrey had sustained a mid-shaft fracture of his right femur. An hour after his admission Pippa had arranged for the theatre to be set up, and a full surgical team were now waiting for Adonis Patras to operate.

Pippa had readily agreed to assist him. She had been, initially, surprised when he asked her, but decided that he was probably trying her out. It was to be her preliminary test, so to speak, and she'd better make a good impression. After a few seconds of nervous apprehension, she told herself that she was perfectly competent to deal with the situation. Having spent a year as Theatre Sister at Benington General, she'd also specialised in orthopaedics during her post-registration year.

Now, as she looked down at the figure beneath the dressing sheet, her thoughts were entirely on the patient. She was thinking that it was difficult to realise that this accident victim was the same healthy young man she'd talked to only yesterday.

'What rotten luck!' she said to Dr Patras as she fixed the Velcro straps at the back of his theatre gown. This was another task he'd insisted she perform; she was sure he was intent on keeping her in her place — which was as hand-maiden to his superior talents — but she would go along with it if it soothed his inflated ego! Her fingers trembled slightly as she pressed against the broad male back. Beneath this thin green cotton there was only firm, tanned skin.

He nodded in agreement with her remark about Geoffrey. 'But it's up to us to make sure we do a good job on Geoffrey's leg. Without work or money, their life in a foreign country isn't going to be much fun. As you say, what rotten luck those two are having.'

This man is human. . .very human, Pippa thought as she watched him turn around and approach the operating-table. Beneath that self-confident exterior he's hiding some very raw emotions. . .compassion for his patient being only one.

The pre-operative discussions of the surgical team stopped and the theatre went deathly quiet. Only the subdued noises of the anaesthetic equipment disturbed the tense atmosphere.

Adonis Patras glanced enquiringly at the anaesthetist. 'Everything OK your end, Jim?'

Jim Burke, a young, fair-haired Australian doctor gave the surgeon a confident smile. 'Excellent, sir.'

The surgeon's eyes above his mask were now fixed on Pippa. With steady, glove-covered fingers grasping her forceps, she held back the sterile dressing sheet that covered the injured leg.

Adonis Patras bent his head to assess the intricate task ahead of him. 'Scalpel, Sister.'

Pippa was surprised to hear the nervousness in Adonis Patras's voice and realised that he was suffering as she was. That was the worst part of becoming involved emotionally with patients. It made the caring of them twice as hard when you knew all that was at stake in their private lives.

She took a deep breath. She mustn't take on the cares of all her patients. The young couple would somehow pull through this bad patch they were going through. And she had to go on and live her own life. She must be professional. . .she mustn't think about the troubles of her patients. . .but it was oh, so hard!

Pippa could see that the reduction of the bone was a particularly difficult one. In her experience she'd found that it was sometimes possible to fix a mid-shaft fracture by closed manipulation. But in Geoffrey's case the bone had broken through the surrounding tissues, causing peripheral damage.

Carefully Adonis Patras fixed the fractured sections of bone in place before repairing the surrounding tissue. He was careful to ensure a satisfactory alignment of the femur, maintaining the natural anterior bowing of the bone and making sure that there was no rotational deformity. Fortunately the thigh muscles appeared unharmed. Next he inserted a Steinmann's pin just behind the tibial tubercle in the knee. This, when used in conjunction with a Thomas's splint and a Pearson's knee flexion piece, would ensure that they could apply the correct amount of traction to hold the limb in place until it was healed.

At the end of the operation Pippa stayed with their patient in the recovery room. As soon as he showed signs of coming round, she removed the airway and called for a porter to help her transport Geoffrey to the orthopaedic unit.

'Has anyone informed Geoffrey's relatives?' Diana Demotis, the capable Greek orthopaedic sister asked Pippa as together the two sisters adjusted the traction on their patient's leg.

Pippa hesitated. 'Our patient has only one relative on Ceres and she's already here in the hospital. . . probably wondering why her boyfriend is taking so

long to collect her. I'd better go and explain the
situation. Will you take over here, Sister? Dr Patras
has requested that a nurse should special Geoffrey for
the first few hours. He'll be along to check on the
traction soon.'

Diana Demotis's smile displayed evenly spaced
small white teeth. 'I'll special our patient myself, Sister
Manson. And I shall be here to assist Dr Patras when
he arrives. I love working with Adonis.'

Pippa gave her colleague a shrewd glance of
appraisal. Mid to late thirties, she thought; probably
one of the long line of the doctor's girlfriends or
would-be girlfriends; probably still smitten by him and
ever hopeful.

Quickly she turned her thoughts back to the patient.
Geoffrey had spoken a few incoherent but encouraging
words before going back to his drug-induced sleep.
His colour was improving; blood-pressure normal
again. She checked his pulse before glancing up at the
IV. He'd lost a fair amount of blood, so he was going
to need a further bottle after this one. She must make
sure it was taken out of the fridge to bring it up to
body temperature.

'I'll be back when I've seen Gina,' she told Diana.
'I'll get the second bottle of blood out before I go.'

'Thanks, Sister.'

What should she say to Gina? she wondered appre-
hensively as she hurried down the corridor. How did
you break bad news to make it acceptable. So many
times in her professional career she'd been faced with
the same problem, and it never got any easier. The
worst situation, she remembered, had been a young
couple whose baby had died during the night, totally
without warning. The strong cups of tea she'd offered

to the distraught parents had been useless in the face of such unutterable grief. When compared with that tragedy, Gina's and Geoffrey's predicament was nothing. At least it could be solved in a few months.

Yes, that was the attitude she should take. If Gina took a positive attitude, she would see that in a year's time all the present problems would have disappeared. She would have a healthy baby; Geoffrey would be fit, well and working.

Taking a deep breath, Pippa pushed open the door to Gina's room and found her sobbing by the window. The news had been broken already.

No amount of philosophical advice was going to stem the torrent of tears, nor soothe away the racking sobs, as Pippa soon realised.

'Can I go and see him?' Gina said, after several minutes of incoherent babbling about how she didn't know where to turn for help and how she couldn't go on any more.

'Tomorrow,' Pippa said gently, as she thought that she would recommend that Gina have some psychiatric counselling. She had been going to arrange it when Gina came to Out-patients, in view of the fact that she'd made an attempt on her life. Whether this was a cry for help or a real attempt, it still pointed to the fact that Gina was unstable at present and needed professional help.

'It's best if you stay on here tonight, Gina,' she told her patient. 'Then in the morning, when Geoffrey is fully round from his anaesthetic, I'll take you along to see him.'

Gina leaned back in the armchair and stared out through the window across the bay. The early afternoon sun was scorching the hillside; a few goats and

sheep wandered across the sparse grass, bleating piti-
fully as they searched for shade.

'I've got nowhere else to go, so I may as well stay,'
she said in a flat tone of defeat. 'That little room down
by the harbour would seem so bare and uncomfortable
without Geoffrey. I shouldn't have come out here,
should I, Sister? I should have stayed at home and
faced the music.'

Pippa took hold of her patient's hand. 'You can't
put the clock back, Gina,' she said gently. 'We all
make mistakes, but life goes on and we go on with it.
It will all turn out for the best. . .you'll see. Now how
about a nice quiet rest in your bed? You've been
awake since dawn, and a sleep would do you and the
baby a lot of good.'

Gina glanced down and patted her tummy. 'Poor
little mite,' she whispered.

'Yes, you've got to take care of your baby now,
Gina,' Pippa said, as she plumped up the pillows
invitingly. 'He can't take care of himself, but you can.'

For a moment a flicker of interest appeared in Gina's
dull eyes. 'Do you think it will be a boy, Sister?'

'It might be. Do you want a boy?'

'I want to go home. . .' The words ended in loud
sobbing.

Pippa gently took hold of the distraught girl and
helped her into bed. 'Sleep now, Gina,' she said softly
as she moved away to check what sedative Adonis
Patras had written up on the chart when Gina had
been admitted. 'A couple of tablets to help you rest.'

Gina took the sedatives and gulped down some
water. Within minutes she was asleep. Pippa tiptoed
out to find a nurse who could stay at the bedside.

'I want you to send for me the moment she wakes up,' she instructed.

'Of course, Sister.'

Pippa walked quickly along the corridor back to the orthopaedic unit to check on Geoffrey. As she reached the door Adonis Patras was coming out.

'How is he?' she asked.

'He's coming round and feeling the pain. I've given him some more pethidine. Diana is specialling him, so we can leave him for a couple of hours. Have you seen Gina?'

Pippa nodded grimly. 'I want to discuss her case with you. It seems to me that ── '

'Let's discuss it over lunch,' he said brusquely. 'It's been a long morning and I'm starving.'

She hesitated as she looked up into the dark brown eyes, but as usual Dr Patras was giving nothing away. It was so difficult to understand this man. One minute he was being the high-handed boss and the next he was suggesting an off-duty meeting.

'This won't be a social occasion,' he added bluntly. 'We need to talk and it's difficult to think when you're hungry.'

He took hold of her arm, steering her off down the corridor, as if she had no say in the matter.

'Just a moment.' She stopped still and faced him. 'I can't leave the hospital. I've told Gina's nurse to send for me the moment she wakes up. I gave her the sedative you wrote up yesterday.'

'I wasn't suggesting we leave the hospital,' he said evenly. 'The cook will find some late lunch for us in the staff dining-room.'

She swallowed hard as she saw the veiled expression of amusement in his eyes. What a *faux pas* she'd made;

imagining the boss was going to take her out to lunch again. But the awful realisation was that, in spite of the objection, she would have enjoyed a taverna lunch with this impossible man.

'Oh, well, in that case. . .' she conceded lamely, turning away so that he couldn't see her embarrassment.

His fingers were under her elbow again, gently ever so gently, but they were there in a proprietorial way. Ostensibly, he was showing her the way to the dining-room, but underneath there was a deeper significance. This man was trying to prove that he could twist her round his little finger, like all the other women in his life. She should be more firm with him, but he was her boss and her job depended on him. Even though her cousin's marriage meant that she was related to the all important Dr Demetrius Capodistrias, it was Dr Patras who was in charge of the day-to-day running of the hospital, and he could make or break her.

The dining-room had a terrace overlooking the harbour. Pippa went out and sat at one of the tables while Adonis Patras went in search of food. All the tables had been cleared and reset for supper. A couple of kitchen staff were preparing vegetables for the evening meal, sitting on stools by the open kitchen door as they tried to get some air. Pippa watched him spreading his hands expressively as he cajoled them into returning to the ancient stoves that ranged the kitchen wall.

'Do you like omelette?' he asked when he returned from the kitchen.

'Is there anything else?'

'No. It's omelette or nothing. Oh, but we can have

some Greek salad with feta cheese and olives. And here comes the bread.'

Petros, the young boy who was the cook's son and helped in the kitchen sometimes after his morning school session to eke out his pocket money, placed a small basket of fresh crusty bread on the table.

'Didn't realise I was so hungry,' Pippa said between mouthfuls of bread and feta cheese.

'Now what were you saying about Gina?' the doctor asked.

'She's going to need some very expert counselling to come through all this,' Pippa replied.

'I know. I've already spoken to Dr Yannis Samos our psychiatrist. I saw him yesterday and he'd agreed to see Gina when she came to Out-patients.'

'I didn't know we had a psychiatrist here. Is there a psychiatric unit?'

Adonis shook his head. 'We rarely need a psychiatrist at the hospital. When we do, I send for Dr Samos to come down from our drug detoxification unit. It's completely separate, up there in the hills.'

He waved his arm towards the sunlit hillside. 'You see at the top there is an old ruined crusaders' castle.'

She shielded her eyes before she could see the impressive ruins that crowned the hilltop overlooking the sea.

'Below the castle there is a new building which houses the drug rehabilitation centre. We take about ten patients at a time and there's always a waiting-list.'

'Who's in charge up there?'

'Dr Samos runs it with voluntary staff who come out for a few months at a time. Alexander Capodistrias started it soon after he smashed the drug organisation who were using this island as one of their bases. It was all very hush-hush, of course, because however many drug organisations you smash there's always another one waiting in the wings. And it can be dangerous to advertise the fact that you've helped the authorities. There are some ruthless types in the drug trade.'

'I'd like to go up there and see the unit,' Pippa said.

Petros arrived with the omelettes and set them down on the table, and Pippa picked up her fork.

'So when can I see the drug detox unit?'

'How about this evening?'

'Fine.'

'Maybe you should take this afternoon off; it could be a strain for you to keep going all day.'

She drew in her breath as she faced him. His enigmatic eyes were watching her; she felt he was willing her to show weakness and give in.

'I'm perfectly capable of doing a full day's work and carrying on into the evening. Your concern is touching . . .but it's a bit late.' Oh, God, she'd gone too far now!

'What do you mean?'

'Nothing.' She started to rise, but he put out a hand to detain her

'No, come on, I insist on an explanation.'

Reluctantly she sat down again. 'I would have thought it obvious what I meant. When I arrived you made it quite clear that you didn't think I was up to the job. You were totally unsympathetic at a time when I needed some reassurance. And now, when I'm getting stronger by the minute, you insist on making out I'm some sort of invalid.'

'Well, aren't you?'

'No. . .could an invalid have worked in Theatre as I

did this morning? Did you have any reason to find fault with me?'

He leaned back in his chair and gave her an expansive smile. 'None whatsoever. I wouldn't have guessed you were suffering in the slightest if I hadn't seen you wriggling out of your shoes in the recovery room.'

'So you were spying on me!'

'I happened to be passing and I remember thinking what a neatly turned ankle you had.'

'Flattery may get you everywhere with some of your staff, Dr Patras but——'

'Look, do you think you could call me Adonis when we're off-duty? I think it would make for a better understanding between us. and I do think we need to understand each other. I admit I had my reservations about your capabilities—and I still have to some extent, because, as I told you, I prefer my staff to be one hundred per cent healthy—but, having said that——'

'I think you've said enough, Adonis,' Pippa broke in, emphasising the doctor's name. 'You've made the situation perfectly clear. I'm on a trial period. If I put a foot wrong. . .pardon the pun,' she interjected with a wry smile, 'you'll have cause for complaint. If you have no cause for complaint I'm sure you'll dream something up.'

As she stood up, she realised that she was trembling with emotion.

'I didn't ask you to come out here. You are free to leave whenever you wish.'

He was towering above her now, his eyes flashing angrily. She'd definitely overstepped the mark this time! But she wasn't one to admit defeat, and the situation intrigued her.

'I don't wish to leave. I like the hospital; I'm enjoying my job. And I'd like to go up to see the detox unit this evening. The more I can learn about the medical facilities on this island the better.'

She walked out of the dining-room, aware, once more, that his eyes followed her. She felt exhausted, but she would keep going. . .all afternoon, all evening, and all night if need be! It was lucky she'd scheduled herself to go off duty at six today. There would be an hour to spare when she could put her feet up and prepare for the evening.

She spent part of the afternoon sorting through the inevitable paperwork that went with her job as administrative sister and then divided the rest of her time between the orthopaedic unit, helping the nurse who was specialling Geoffrey, and the obstetric unit, caring for Gina.

As soon as she went off duty she hurried to her room, took off her shoes, and eased hereslf out of her uniform. Flat on the bed, she closed her eyes and took a few deep breaths. Mmm, that was lovely. Simply to relax. . . She mustn't fall asleep. . .

The shrilling of the phone brought her back to the present and she realised that she'd been in danger of dropping off.

'Nicole!' Her cousin's voice was instantly recognisable.

'Is everything going OK, Pippa?'

'Fine!'

'And is it what you expected? I mean I hope you're spending your time in the office with your feet up. You can delegate from there. We're a well staffed hospital and there's no need for you to run around. Not until you feel up to it. Is that how it's working out?'

Pippa hesitated. 'Not exactly. I mean, I don't think it would go down too well with. . .' Pippa broke off, wondering just how much she dared confide in Nicole. Cousin or no cousin, she was still the wife of the director of this hospital, who'd appointed Adonis Patras in the first place and who was a personal friend.

'With whom, Pippa?' Nicole persisted.

Well, better get it over with! 'Adonis Patras made it quite clear that he thought my appointment was a mistake.'

Pippa heard the intake of breath at the other end.

'Ah, yes; to be honest, Pippa, this is why I'm calling. I thought he might kick up a fuss. But I hoped that once you'd arrived there would be no problem. I mean, in your own office you can be your own boss and——'

'Nicole, I've no intention of sitting in my office all day. And anyway, Dr Patras asked me to assist in Theatre this morning. I think he was hoping I'd duck out, but I didn't.'

'So it's out-and-out war, is it? Oh, Pippa, I'm so sorry to land you in this situation. Look, if it gets too bad give me a call. I'll ask Alexander to intervene and appoint Ariadne Stangos temporarily. You could spend some time relaxing round at the house in Symborio and then go back to England.'

'I'm going to see this through, Nicole. I like the hospital and I know I can do the job. So don't worry.'

'Well, call me if you can't take any more. Adonis Patras can be very stubborn. He's used to getting his own way.'

'You can say that again!'

Nicole went on to ask about her father-in-law. Pippa

gave all the details of her visit before Nicole had to
end the conversation.

Pippa got off the bed and went for a shower. She
looked in the wardrobe for a clean uniform. In this hot
climate it was only possible to wear the blue dress for
a few hours. She found that the maid had been in and
reorganised her clothes, placing a brand new uniform
at the front.

She found no difficulty in walking with a firm step to
the reception area of the hospital. Adonis Patras was
waiting by the main entrance, car keys in hand.

'Good evening, Adonis,' she said blandly. She
would start as she meant to go on this evening. He'd
asked her to call him Adonis and she would try to
remember. It was a step in the right direction towards
their *entente cordiale*.

The sun had set, but the warmth of the day still
lingered as Adonis drove the Land Rover up the
narrow, newly metalled road, twisting and twining
through the terraced hillside. Pippa leaned back
against the hard seat, trying to shake off the fatigue
that had been chasing her since late afternoon. It had
been a long day, starting with the early morning swim
at Symborio, and then coping with Geoffrey's emergency operation and post-operative care.

As she glanced out of the open window of the car
her weariness began to lift. Up here among the sheep
and the goats and the herb-scented hillsides was a
perfect place for rehabilitation. She could see one
reason why the area had been chosen for the detox
unit. . .the sheer beauty of the place. And the other
would be the need to keep a low profile and a certain
amount of anonymity.

'How was Gina when she woke up?' Adonis asked

as he negotiated a particularly difficult hairpin bend. He straightened his arms around the steering-wheel and glanced briefly at Pippa.

'Much calmer, but she certainly needs help. We can't tell what she's thinking when she's been sedated. I've asked the night staff to be as helpful as possible, but to keep a watchful eye in case she tries anything dangerous.'

'Exactly. Well, you'll meet Dr Samos in a few minutes and we'll ask his advice.'

The detoxification unit was housed in a newly renovated building beneath the ramparts of the castle. In the gathering darkness it looked bright and inviting with lights shining out from every open window.

'Come in and welcome,' Dr Samos said as they arrived at the open door.

Yannis Samos was a small man in his mid to late forties, a twinkling smile on his face which was reflected in his dark brown sypathetic eyes.

'I cannot give you a beer or wine, my friends. We have only fruit juice up here.'

'Fruit juice will be fine,' Adonis said as he followed his colleague through into a small courtyard.

Dr Samos ushered them towards some wooden chairs set beside an ancient carved table.

'Be seated, my friends.'

Pippa watched the kindly Greek doctor signalling to a servant, who arrived soon afterwards with a tray of glasses and a large jug of orange juice, the ice cubes clinking invitingly.

Pippa was hot and decidedly weary after her long day, so she drank quickly before setting her glass down on the gnarled old table. She glanced across the courtyard to where Dr Samos was speaking with his servant, instructing him to bring out some *mezes*, little dishes of assorted Greek food. The doctor stepped out of the shadows and moved back across the courtyard.

The young serving boy brought out the plates of *mezes* and placed them on the old table. There was crusty Greek bread and dishes of taramasalata, tzatziki, large, juicy tomatoes, baked aubergines, yoghurt pâté and bitter black olives. They talked as they helped themselves to the delicious spread.

'Our patient, Gina, is going to need your help, Yannis,' Adonis said, his dark eyes fixed on the psychiatric expert.

Dr Samos glanced down at the notes Adonis had prepared for him. 'You say Gina tried to kill herself. Was it a real attempt or a cry for help?'

'You're the expert,' Adonis replied. 'We'd like you to decide. When can you come down to the hospital to see Gina?'

'I'll come tomorrow morning. From what you've told me, it's important for Gina to start her treatment at once.'

They discussed the case at length as the evening darkened. Pippa looked out across the mountain slope towards the sea. The twinkling lights of Kato, the lower town, beckoned and she could hear the music of a bouzouki drifting out from the taverna in Epano, the old, partially ruined upper town not too far away from them.

The magic of a Greek night! she thought as they packed up their files and prepared to leave their amiable host. Her feet were itching to dance to the tantalising rhythm of Greek music, and with a pang she realised that it would be several weeks more before her injured foot was strong enough to give her the balance she needed for dancing. But meanwhile there were lots of other activities she could enjoy in her off duty time on this idyllic island. She could do more swimming. There was no problem with the injured foot when she was in the water.

It was getting late, but she decided that she ought to check on Geoffrey and Gina when she got back to hospital. She was officially off-duty, but it would only take a few minutes.

'I'd like to have a look around the rest of the unit some time when it's convenient,' Pippa said, 'to meet the patients and so on. It's rather late to disturb them now. I expect some of them will be asleep.'

Dr Samos nodded. 'We'll fix another time that's mutually convenient, Sister. Perhaps you would telephone me in the near future. One thing I must stress is that some of our patients don't want any publicity. There are a few who have been famous in the world of show business. Some have been respected members of their community back in the UK and the United States. They are able to come out here, and their friends and colleagues simply think they are taking a long holiday on a remote island. So we have to respect their privacy.'

'But of course,' Pippa said hastily. 'That goes without saying.' She found herself warming to this sensitive, benevolent doctor, whose sole concern was for the welfare of his patients. She was glad she'd visited the unit, and she would certainly return at a later date when she had more time to spare. Meanwhile she could rest assured that the detox unit was in excellent hands.

'It's time we were getting back to the hospital,' Adonis put in.

'Thank you for the refreshments, Dr Samos,' Pippa said.

'It was my pleasure, my dear,' the doctor said in a benign tone.

They shook hands and went out into the starlit night. The moon was shining brightly on the herb-scented hillside. The warmth of the day still hung in the velvet air. As they reached the Land Rover, turning to look once more at the strange building, Pippa saw a star shooting across the sky. Then it began to fall, swiftly, zooming towards the ground.

She felt Adonis's hand on her waist as he helped her up into the Land Rover.

'Why don't you make a wish, Philippa,' he said, smiling. 'Catch the falling star before it lands.'

She drew in her breath. Adonis's eyes were level with her own and she could see his expression of amusement.

She laughed as she closed her eyes. 'What shall I wish, I wonder? Now let me see. . .'

The strangest wish had come into her mind. She didn't want even to think about it. . .but it was there. And if it came true. . .

She opened her eyes and looked at Adonis. His face was very close to hers and the smile had vanished, to be replaced by an enigmatic expression that she couldn't understand.

'What did you wish?' he asked quietly.

'It has to be a secret,' she replied in a bantering tone.

A strange spell seemed to fall on her, holding her quite still. This man, this unknown quantity, was no longer a stranger, no longer her enemy. She was in a state of truce with him. . . More than that, she found herself attracted to him. But it was a dangerous situation. If she allowed herself to be lulled into a false sense of security with him, how could she be sure he wouldn't turn on her and reveal his unsympathetic side again? She looked around her at the dark trees surrounding the Land Rover. They were quite alone.

She leaned back against her seat, feeling a deep sense of peace stealing over her.

'You must love this island, Adonis.' She realised this was the first time she'd said his name without feeling self-conscious.

'Oh, I do. This was where I spent my summers as a boy.'

'And do you return here every summer?'

'Not now. My father used to come here from our house in Athens until health prevented him from travelling. But now he is very sick and remains at home. My mother died many years ago, so he is cared for by professional nurses who live in the house.'

'What is the. . .?' She hesitated before continuing. 'What is the medical problem?'

'Carcinoma of the bronchus. . .secondaries in the lung. It's only a question of time,' he replied in a dead-pan tone.

Pippa drew in her breath. 'I'm so sorry, Adonis. But shouldn't you be with your father?' she asked in concern.

'My father receives visitors by appointment. When he sends for me I will go.'

'But you're his son!'

'Years ago, my father and I had. . .' He hesitated before continuing. 'Let's say we had a difference of opinion. My father has never forgiven me.'

'And yet you care enough for him to put aside your

own happiness by going along with a betrothal of
convenience.' The words escaped before she had considered what she was saying.

Adonis frowned. 'I see you've been listening to
Ariadne Stangos. She loves to gossip. Some of it is
true; some of it is not. You can make your own
judgement. In the strictest confidence I will tell you
that you are right when you say my betrothal to
Cassiopi is one of convenience, duty to my family. . .'
He broke off, a veiled expression crossing his eyes, as
if regretting the admission. 'This is a confidence,
Philippa, but if we are to work together more har-
moniously it will perhaps help to explain some of the
problems in my life. Because where my father is
concerned I know only that he is my father and
therefore must be respected. After all, family is
family.'

She felt out of her depth. Adonis was revealing a
side of his character that she hadn't suspected.

'We must go back to the hospital,' she urged quietly.

He leaned towards her and ran a finger down the
side of her cheek. She felt the ecstatic *frisson* of contact
with this enigmatic man. For one uncertain moment
she thought he was going to kiss her. His parted lips
were so very close to hers, but suddenly he turned
away and put his hands back on the wheel.

The engine of the Land Rover sprang to life and
they were hurtling off down the rough track back to
the hospital.

CHAPTER SIX

TIME passed quickly for Pippa as she threw herself whole-heartedly into her new job. She was used to being totally committed to her professional medical duties, but her distractingly uncertain relationship with Adonis made her even more determined to work hard. When she was working she had no time to worry about it.

A whole month had passed in what seemed like a few days, during which Pippa's hospital duties had been totally absorbing and she had gained a good rapport with the nursing staff. She'd aimed at achieving a friendly but firm relationship with all the nurses and, as she reviewed the situation on a hot Monday morning in June, she hoped that she was achieving what she'd set out to do.

'*Efharisto* — thank you. That's all the letters for this morning, Elena,' she told her medical secretary.

'*Efharisto*.' The elderly Greek woman smiled and gathered up her papers. '*Kahnee zehstee seemehrah*.'

Pippa agreed that it certainly was hot today. And for some reason the overhead ceiling fan had seemed ineffective during the morning's work as she'd struggled with Greek and English letters and case histories. Elena was a great help, but Pippa had to make all the decisions, which wasn't easy in this temperature.

She realised that she was at her happiest when working among the patients, where she didn't notice

the heat so much. Most of the medical and surgical
units kept their windows wide open and there was
always a cool breeze from the sea. But her own office
faced into the courtyard, and there wasn't a breath of
air.

She stood up and stretched as Elena went out and
closed the door. That was better! To be able to move
about. Thank goodness she hadn't decided to take that
secretarial course that her mother had suggested.
Office work was so boring!

She walked across to the window and stared out
across the bay to the mountain slopes beyond. She
could imagine the scent of the herbs and the beauty of
the rugged valleys beyond the mountain. One day she
must go there. Her injured foot was strengthening and
she would soon be able to go over the uneven ground
without worrying about stumbling and hurting herself.

'You're looking very solemn!'

Pippa swung round from the window at the sound of
Ariadne Stangos's voice.

'I did knock before I came in, Sister, but you were
lost in thought, I expect. You've been looking far too
pensive lately. Got a problem, have you?'

Pippa looked across the room at the older woman,
who was now ensconced in one of the armchairs where
consultations with patients' relatives often took place,
and she reflected that she'd come to value Ariadne's
friendship. At the back of her mind there was always
the niggling doubt, put there by Adonis, that Ariadne
was only interested in gossiping, and that anything she
said would be spread around the hospital grapevine,
but so far Pippa had found her friend to be totally
trustworthy.

She crossed to the consultation area and sank down into one of the armchairs.

'No, I haven't got a problem with the work here, Ariadne. Everything is under control and I'm glad I'm doing this job.'

'Well, the nursing staff like the way you're running things,' Ariadne smiled. 'And they respect you, which is the main thing. In fact I think dear old Sister Arama will have a bad time taking up the reins again when she gets back from America with Dr Capodistrias and your cousin Nicole. I don't suppose you've thought of staying on after October. Sister Arama was contemplating retirement, and if you were around it might make up her mind.'

Pippa sighed. 'To be honest, Ariadne, I've no idea what I'm going to do when this contract finishes. The possibilities are endless, but——'

'But it's difficult to make decisions when you're in the middle of a tough assignment, isn't that right?'

Pippa hesitated. 'It's just so hard to work out whether Dr Patras approves of my work or not. He can be so difficult. I know it shouldn't matter; I mean, I know I'm doing a good job and you've just told me that the rest of the hospital like the way I'm doing things, so why should I be so sensitive where one doctor is concerned? He can be so infuriating! He seems to take pride in belittling me whenever he can, making out that I came here for a rest cure, which I certainly did not!'

Ariadne leaned forward. 'I would say that the problem is you care too much about him. You value his opinion too highly. And, to be honest, I think the reason he picks on you is because he's attracted to you and he's trying to cover up.'

'Oh, don't be silly!'

'Whenever I see the two of you together, I marvel at the self-control. I can see the electric current running between you.'

'More like sparks flying!' Pippa retorted.

'You're both holding back from your true feelings because you, Pippa, are still peeved that he tried to obstruct your appointment and you daren't trust him not to object again, and Adonis is committed to Cassiopi, so he's not free.'

'Well, thank you for the psychological diagnosis! Honestly, Ariadne, you must have the most fertile imagination.'

'Be honest with yourself, Pippa. Can you truthfully say you don't find Adonis attractive?'

'Of course I find him attractive in the same way that any sane woman confronted with a gorgeous hunk of manhood would do. I mean you find him attractive — don't you? — but I don't accuse you of wanting to. . .' She broke off, realising that her tongue was running away with her.

'Wanting to what, Pippa?'

Pippa hesitated. 'Wanting to get to know him better, I suppose.'

She ran her hands through her hair. She still hadn't had it cut, because she'd heard Adonis saying he liked long hair.

'I've lost you again,' Ariadne said. 'Penny for them.'

Pippa smiled. 'Well, as you say, even if someone was attracted to Adonis it wouldn't do them any good, because there's another woman waiting in the wings. I would imagine Cassiopi keeps a tight rein on him.'

For the second time that morning the door had

opened without Pippa realising it. Adonis stood on the threshold, a quizzical expression on his face.

'I'd like to come in if I'm not breaking up the hen-party,' he said in a dry tone.

Pippa's pulses were racing. 'Do come in. Sister Stangos was just leaving.'

Ariadne jumped to her feet and made for the door. As she passed Adonis she looked up and gave him a knowing smile.

Pippa felt a wave of apprehension sweeping over her. Ariadne and Adonis were part of a totally different culture. They'd grown up together. . .along with Cassiopi. How could she hope to understand the situation here? How could she even contemplate romance with a man who had a past. . .and probably no future? Certainly not with her, at any rate.

As the door closed on Ariadne, Pippa got up and walked over to the window, standing with her back towards Adonis so that he wouldn't guess at the turmoil of her feelings.

'I don't like to think that the staff are discussing my private life,' she heard him say in careful, measured tones. 'I confided in you about my relationship with Cassiopi and I hoped the confidence would remain secret.'

She swung round to face him, her eyes blazing. 'What have you told me about your relationship with Cassiopi except that it's a sham? But why should I believe you?'

'Why indeed? Anyway, Cassiopi has gone to America for a few weeks to stay with relatives,' he replied in a dead-pan tone.

'Are you implying this makes you a free man?'

'I have always been a free man,' he replied in a

dangerously controlled voice. 'I'm merely constrained
by a business arrangement between our families.'

'But Ariadne told me that everyone is convinced
you will marry Cassiopi. . .'

'Ariadne talks too much. You mustn't confide in
her.'

Pippa walked back to her desk and sat down, proud
of the fact that her steps had been firm and steady.
'Did you want to see me about a hospital matter or
was this just a social call?'

He leaned towards her across the desk. 'Both. I
want you to come with me now to talk to Gina about
her arrangements for the birth of her baby. She's in
the orthopaedic unit, visiting Geoffrey. And then I
want you to take the afternoon off and let me show
you some of the beauty of this island.'

'What brought this on?' she asked warily.

'I've been watching the way you walk and I think
you'll cope now with the rigours of the Greek land-
scape. We're justifiably proud of our beautiful island
of Ceres and I'd like to share it with you. You are a
guest on our island and I've decided that perhaps I
was — what shall we say? — a little inhospitable when
you first arrived.'

Pippa drew in her breath. 'A little? Yes, I agree
with you there. But. . .' She waved her hands over the
pile of case-notes. 'I'm having a blitz on my paper-
word. I've been concentrating too much on practical
work in the hospital and neglecting the organisation.
So today I planned to — '

'Today I planned to show you the island, and I won't
take no for an answer.'

She hesitated. 'I suppose this could wait until

tomorrow, and I've given Elena a lot of work to do, so perhaps——'

'Of course it can wait. It's only the patients whose needs have to be taken care of, and I assure you the hospital is very quiet at the moment. We're positively overstaffed.'

Pippa stood up. 'OK. Let's go and see Gina and Geoffrey.'

Sister Diana Demotis was adjusting the weights that controlled the traction on Geoffrey's leg. She smiled up at Adonis as he and Pippa reached the bedside.

'How's Geoffrey, Sister?' Adonis asked, picking up and glancing quickly at the charts.

'He's doing fine, Doctor. These are the latest X-rays. Perhaps Sister Manson would like to see them too.'

'I certainly would.' Pippa leaned forward as Adonis held the X-rays to the light.

Adonis traced his finger across the mid-shaft fracture of the right femur. 'See where the healing process has started?'

Pippa nodded. 'It's looking very healthy.'

She moved to the head of the bed and smiled down at their patient. 'You're doing fine, Geoffrey.'

'Yes, but when can I come off this wretched contraption?' He waved his arms in the direction of the traction. 'I want to get out and make some money for Gina and the child.'

'You'll have to be patient, Geoffrey,' Adonis said. 'It's going to take a few more weeks, but we should have you out of here before the baby's born.'

'I should hope so. October's a long way off. But we

want to get married before the baby comes,' Geoffrey said. 'And we can't get married if I'm stuck in here.'

'Why not?' Adonis said. 'We could arrange a wedding in hospital. And don't worry about money, Geoffrey. We'll sort something out.'

'Do you really mean we could have a wedding in hospital?' Gina put in. So far she had taken a back seat in all the proceedings, remaining quietly beside the bed, but now her decidedly animated expression showed that she was coming out of the depression.

Pippa felt relieved to see the look of interest on Gina's face. After a month of counselling in Outpatients with Dr Samos, Gina was beginning to show a more positive attitude towards life.

'Would you like to be married here, Gina?' Adonis asked.

Gina hesitated. 'I'm sure Geoffrey would.'

'Yes, but what about you, Gina?' Pippa persisted.

Again the hesitation. 'I'm not sure.'

'Ye gods, woman!'

Pippa had never seen Adonis so moved to anger by a patient. His usually calm professional exterior had cracked and she saw beneath it to the passionate, hot-blooded man she had come to admire against her own wishes. She knew that Gina's total lack of romantic commitment to Geoffrey was irritating Adonis to the point where he could no longer stand back and play the detached professional doctor.

'Why can't you think of Geoffrey for once?' Adonis said heatedly. 'This man wants to devote his life to you and your unborn child and all you can do is sit on the fence and moan about what might have been.'

'I'm not sure Dr Samos would approve,' Pippa whispered under her breath to Adonis.

'To hell with Dr Samos! All this pussyfooting around for a situation that's as old as the hills,' Adonis retorted. He took hold of the startled Gina's hands and bent down towards her so that his eyes were level with her face. 'Do you think you're the only girl who ever got pregnant before marriage? Do you?'

'No, I suppose——'

'You suppose correctly, my girl. And what you've got to do is face facts. Your man is asking you to marry him, here in the hospital. So what do you say? Shall I go ahead and arrange a wedding for you?'

Gina's answer was barely audible, but it was definitely a yes.

'And then we must decide where you will live,' Pippa put in quickly. 'The little room you're renting will be too small after the baby is born. There's a small apartment at the side of the hospital, used by families of our hospital porters. There's no one in it at the moment, because our porters are all from the island and living in their family homes. I could arrange for you to move in, because Geoffrey will be a porter here as soon as his leg heals. If you were settled in before the baby was born, Gina, you would be literally on the doorstep for the actual birth. You could come into the hospital for a few hours and then return to your apartment as soon as you were fit.'

Gina's eyes widened with disbelief. 'You mean we could have a whole apartment to ourselves?'

'It's not very big,' Pippa said quickly. 'Just a bedroom, living-room with a kitchenette and a small shower-room. But it's in good condition—brand new in fact, because we haven't needed to use it before.'

'But what about the rent?' Geoffrey asked nervously. 'I can't pay while I'm lying here.'

Pippa looked across at Adonis. They'd had to pull a few strings and speak to old Dr Demetrius, but a solution had been found.

'You're on the payroll already, Geoffrey,' Adonis said, 'so the apartment goes with the job, and you'll receive sick-pay until you can start work for us.'

Geoffrey's lip quivered. 'You're very kind. I don't know how I'll ever repay you.'

'Just get better. . .that's all we ask,' Pippa said slowly. 'And the wedding will go ahead as soon as we can make the arrangements. Gina and I will get together and work everything out when Dr Patras has spoken to the priest.'

Pippa and Adonis left Gina and Geoffrey to discuss the impending wedding. Pippa was relieved to see the interest that Gina was at last beginning to show.

'I hope we're doing the right thing,' she said to Adonis as they walked down the corridor towards the main entrance of the hospital. 'Dr Samos might think it psychologically unsound to direct our patients' course of action.'

Adonis stopped still in the middle of the corridor and put his hand on Pippa's arm to detain her. 'Stop worrying about Gina and Geoffrey. What we've suggested to them is the only workable solution to the problem. We're doing what we think is right for them. They're not going to have an easy time, whatever course of action we take, and I happen to think that those two young lovers will fall in love all over again when they set up house in their little love nest.'

Pippa smiled. 'I hadn't realised you were such a romantic, Adonis. I do believe you think that love makes the world go round, don't you?'

Adonis put a finger under her chin and tilted her

face upwards so that they were looking into each other's eyes. 'Yes, I do. . .but I believe it's important to find the right person. So far. . .'

But he didn't finish his sentence as Jim Burke, the Australian doctor, rounded the corner from Outpatients, and the two of them carried on walking down the corridor. Pippa longed to know what Adonis had been about to say. So far, had he had no luck in finding the right person?

'There's an emergency appendicectomy due in Theatre in ten minutes, sir,' Jim Burke said breathlessly. 'I was told I could find you in Orthopaedics.

'But Dr Seferis was in Theatre this morning. I thought he was going to add the appendix to his list,' Adonis said.

'He's still not fully recovered from that viral infection he had and he's feeling tired. He asked me to request that you do the emergency for him.'

'Yes, of course.' Adonis quickened his stride as he went off with Dr Burke, turning only briefly to speak to Pippa.

'I'll see you in your office about two, Sister, in connection with our island research.'

She saw the mischievous grin on Adonis's unbelievably boyish face and smiled back.

At two o'clock she was waiting in her office, having changed out of her uniform into cream linen trousers and a white polo shirt. In her capacious duffel bag she had a bikini, a pair of shorts and a towel, because she had no idea what kind of an expedition this 'research' of the island would entail.

When Adonis came into her office he was wearing blue denim jeans that moulded to his muscular thighs, a cotton shirt opened almost to the waist, revealing dark hairs on his tanned chest, and, instead of his usual stethoscope, a cashmere sweater was knotted loosely around his neck.

As she stood up, brushing aside the papers, she could feel the butterflies churning away in the pit of her stomach.

'Are you ready, Pippa?'

She glanced towards the duffel bag. 'I've packed something to swim in. . . I didn't know what exactly we —'

'Fine. Let's go before someone tries to offload their work on us. As I said, the hospital is positively overstaffed, but if we're around we'll be made to work. There's nothing going on that the staff can't handle this afternoon. My emergency appendicectomy is recovering well and Nick Seferis is feeling fit again and has asked to take over.'

'Dr Seferis has been here for a few years, hasn't he?' Pippa observed. 'I remember my cousin Nicole talking about him when she first came out. I believe she found him most helpful.'

'Yes, I think he arrived here newly qualified around the time Nicole started work in the hospital. He's an excellent doctor, but he's been run down recently after a holiday in the Far East, where he went down with a viral infection. He's over the worst, but he gets tired easily. I offered him extended sick-leave but he insisted on returning to work.'

Adonis picked up Pippa's duffel bag in one hand and pulled her towards the door with the other.

'Let's escape while we can,' he said, smiling down at her. 'There's a lot of research to be done.'

* * *

Pippa lay stretched out on deck, shielded from the sun by a canvas awning. In one hand she held a long, cold glass of fresh orange juice, swirling with twists of mint, tiny segments of lemon and tinkling with ice cubes, while the other hand trailed lazily in the warm water.

This is the life! she thought as she smiled across at Adonis, who was sprawled across the other end of the deck. They had changed into swim things, not so much in preparation for a swim as to allow the maximum cooling effect from the sea breezes as the three members of the sailing crew negotiated the boat around the coast of Ceres. Adonis had explained that Alexander Capodistrias had very generously offered him full use of his boat, complete with crew, while he was away in the States.

She raised herself on to her elbows and peered across the heat-hazed sea towards the rocky coastline. parse grass intermingling with granite rocks, inhabited only by sheep and goats, sheered down to the sea. The coastline was indented occasionally, with tall, straight cliffs guarding the entrance to dark, mysterious bays where the sun penetrated for only a few hours each day.

Pippa yawned and gave a lazy smile. 'I suppose I should be taking notes on our round trip of the island,' she said. 'What's that white building over there on the top of the hill?'

Adonis sat up. 'That's the church of Ayios Filimonos. There are many churches on the island, but some of them are difficult to reach. There are ill defined tracks that go between the churches, but often it's easier to go by sea. We're going to stop at one of the churches — Ayios Emilianos; it's in a beautiful bay where we can swim.' He hesitated before asking, 'Do you like our island of Ceres, Pippa?'

'I love it,' she replied ingenuously. 'I'm completely captivated by everything I've seen this afternoon.'

He moved towards her. 'And when we land the crew will prepare a barbecue while we swim.'

For a fleeting second she wondered how many girls Adonis had brought out here. Well, that was no concern of hers. She was simply going to enjoy the afternoon and her boss's change of heart towards her.

They were rounding a headland and there was a view of a warm, sunlit bay with a dazzlingly white church set on a narrow peninsula.

Adonis spoke to the crew and the boat headed for land.

Pippa felt the excitement rising inside her. It was like going to a desert island. She'd never been anywhere so remote.

She glanced up at the tantalising man beside her. The sun was crowning his head with its rays, and for a second she could imagine he was a Greek god come down from Mount Olympus. She found herself hoping that his relationship with Cassiopi really was purely a convenience, because it would be very easy to fall in love with a man like this. . .if he were free.

CHAPTER SEVEN

THE crew were busying themselves with preparations for the barbecue, carrying boxes of food and utensils from the boat before lighting a charcoal fire on the rocky promontory that jutted out into the sea.

'Let's swim first,' Adonis said, as he dived over the side of the boat.

Pippa checked the straps of her white bikini before following Adonis into the water. Down, down, down she went, marvelling at the sheer depth of the bay and the kaleidoscope of colour under the sea. There were fish of all shapes and sizes swimming alongside, apparently undisturbed at the intrusion of the land creatures. She swam towards the shore again and put out her hand to touch the velvety vegetation that covered the surface of one of the submerged rocks.

'Be careful; there are sea urchins, whose prickles are dangerous if they stick in your skin.'

She heard Adonis's voice from somewhere on the surface and pulled herself out into the strong sunlight.

'But it's like a magic kingdom down there. All we need is Poseidon with his trident, sitting on his throne.'

'And you would make a beautiful mermaid,' Adonis said gently, his hand reaching out to touch the long, wet strands of her hair.

She laughed as she pulled away, trying to make light of a gesture that had moved her more than she cared to admit. 'Race you back to the shore!'

He was beside her in the water, thrusting his arms

in muscular actions that churned up the sea. He appeared to be swimming as fast as he could, but Pippa knew he could beat her if he chose to race on ahead.

'Dead heat!' he called, as they pulled themselves up on to a smooth, dry rock, warmed by the sunshine.

She pulled her hair back from her face and lay down, basking in the hot rays of the sun. Yes, today she felt like a mermaid, a creature without the cares of the world. Today she felt the enchantment of being with Adonis more strongly than ever before.

Be careful, said the cold voice of reason inside her head. Remember, you'll only get hurt if he really is committed to Cassiopi.

The crew had finished cooking and were signalling for Adonis and Pippa to come over to the wooden table they'd erected beside the sea.

They went back on board the boat as soon as Adonis and Pippa had settled themselves in the comfortable canvas chairs beside the table. Pippa looked around the goodies spread out before her. There was barbe-cued chicken scented with oregano, red mullet, large king prawns, green olives and a Greek salad.

'Did you organise all this?' she asked, looking across the table at Adonis.

He smiled as he picked up a chicken drumstick and began to devour it hungrily. 'Let's say I instructed the crew what to buy. They've been with the Capodistrias family for a long time, so they've done this before. I remember coming out here with Alexander Capodistrias and a crowd of friends when we were all much younger.'

'Was Cassiopi there?' she asked, trying to sound unconcerned.

'Maybe; I really can't remember.'

She began to peel a prawn. Some of the excitement had died as her thoughts had turned to Cassiopi. She couldn't help wondering if Cassiopi was in love with Adonis. How could she not be? And if so, Pippa felt she had no right to contemplate a relationship with Adonis.

'You're worrying about something. Tell me what's troubling you.'

She raised her head and faced him. 'I was thinking about Cassiopi. . . I shouldn't be here with you, Adonis. Cassiopi——'

'We're having a harmless picnic together. I'm showing you a little of our famous Greek hospitality. Besides, Cassiopi has her own affair to console her,' Adonis interrupted tersely. 'At this very moment she is with her lover in New York.'

Pippa's eyes widened in disbelief. 'But how do you know?'

Adonis put down his fork and leaned back in his chair. 'Because she told me. But you are the only one who knows this besides myself. I trust you to keep this secret. The families would be desolate if they knew.'

Pippa shook her head. 'I don't understand the situation at all. Are you trying to tell me that both you and Cassiopi are pretending to go along with this sham of a betrothal?'

Adonis glanced warily across at the boat, but the sailors were all below in the cabin. 'That's exactly what I'm saying. . .but no one must know. Promise me, Philippa, that you won't breathe a word to a living soul.'

She took a deep breath. 'I promise. You have my word.'

She was touched by his confidence in her, and a

great weight seemed to have been lifted from her shoulders. If this was true, then Adonis would eventually be free of this mysterious family commitment which, apparently, neither he nor Cassiopi had wanted to agree to.

At last she felt like eating the delicious food. Adonis passed over a large china serving dish of mullet, and she chose a succulent fish to accompany her prawns as a starter. He poured some champagne into her lead crystal glass.

The sun was halfway into the water as they finished their meal. Adonis got up from his chair, came round the table, and held out his hand.

'Come to the edge of the bay, by the church, so we can see the sunset.'

As she took hold of his outstretched hand she felt a wild shiver of anticipation running down her spine. They left the table and ran over the warm rocks to the ancient white church. The sun's rays were darting over the land, giving it an orange glow in these final moments of the day. And then the fiery ball disappeared below the surface of the water and only a dim light remained.

'That was beautiful,' Pippa murmured, half to herself.

She remained totally still as Adonis's arm slid around her bare shoulder. And then, very gently, he cupped her face with his hands and kissed her. She held her breath as their lips blended together for a few tender moments.

'I love the magic hour of the sunset,' he said huskily. 'It heralds the beginning of the night, with all its mysteries. Over there on the water you can see —'

'*Ghiatros*! *Ghiatros*!'

Adonis frowned as he heard one of the sailors calling to him from the boat. Pippa had noticed that the crew always spoke in Greek and addressed Adonis with the Greek word for doctor. But she had heard Adonis giving instructions that they weren't to be disturbed except for a dire emergency.

The sailor was now running towards them, his bare feet skimming the rocky surface.

From the rapid Greek conversation that followed Pippa was able to deduce that a message had come over the boat's radio.

'What is it, Adonis?' she asked as they followed the sailor back to the boat.

'It's Nick Seferis,' he replied grimly. 'He's collapsed. Jim Burke has taken charge of the hospital, but he's worried about Nick's condition.'

'Is it a recurrence of the viral infection he had in the Far East?'

Adonis drew in his breath. 'From what I've heard, it sounds as if this so-called viral infection could be malaria.'

Pippa put a hand over her mouth in an involuntary gesture of horror. 'Oh, no! But can we deal with malaria at the hospital?'

'We'll have to!' was Adonis's determined reply. 'But let's wait until we've examined Nick. I could be wrong. It's difficult to make a diagnosis when you're several miles away from the patient.'

As the boat sped back to Kato Town around the coastline, Pippa insisted that Adonis refresh her memory about the signs, symptoms and treatment of malaria. She told him that she'd only touched briefly on tropical diseases during her nursing training and she'd never actually nursed a case.

They were sitting in the cabin. A lamp had been lit on the table. The atmosphere was cosy, but the tension between them was purely professional again. They had no thought of anything except their patient.

'In my opinion, Nick suffered a mild form of malaria while he was out in the Far East. This has now returned in a stronger manifestation. An attack of malaria usually consists of three stages — a stage of coldness, a stage of heat, and a stage of sweating — followed by an interval when the symptoms appear to have subsided. Apparently Nick had suffered the three stages in a mild form since returning to the hospital, but he's been dosing himself with chloroquine and hoping to cure himself without worrying the rest of us. The malarial cycle has now returned and he's desperately cold and unable to get out of bed.'

'How awful. But he's not infectious, is he?'

Adonis shook his head. 'Malaria is contracted when you're bitten by an anopheline mosquito which has previously fed on the blood of an infected person. We shall be quite safe when we take care of Nick, and he's no danger to our patients, except if he decides to continue working when he's not fit. I simply cannot understand why medical staff do this! An unfit nurse or doctor is a menace to the hospital!'

'I think you've made yourself clear about that before,' Pippa said quietly.

'And I stick by my opinion,' he continued heatedly. 'Medical staff who think they must continue at all costs should be reprimanded.'

Pippa drew in her breath at the harshness of his pronouncement. 'You've made your point, now leave it. I know you disapproved of me coming out here, but it's sometimes necessary for —'

'It's never necessary! I've known mistakes to be made, patients to be put in danger——'

'But there are exceptions to your rule. When I came out here I was totally fit except for my foot. The unfortunate incident when I arrived set me back a bit, but I soon recovered—no thanks to you!' She broke off and took a deep breath, knowing she'd gone too far and cursing herself for breaking up the rapport that had been building up all afternoon.

'Let's just stick to the task in hand and remain objective,' he said coldly. 'It's Nick Seferis we're concerned about. The fact that you've aquitted yourself favourably so far doesn't mean that you're out of the wood. What would happen if you stumbled when you were carrying a baby?'

'I wouldn't! I'm perfectly steady on my feet now. And besides, I'm extra cautious when I carry the babies. I'm aware that. . .that there could be a problem if I. . .' She broke off, realising that she was playing into his hand.

'Exactly! You're aware, just as I'm aware, that——'

'You're twisting my words.' But even as she said it she knew she'd lost the contest. And she'd lost the man. She ought to hate him, but instead their word-sparring had only increased her attraction towards him.

'Let's concentrate on the patient,' he snapped. 'This is no time for histrionics.'

She bit her lip and willed herself to be silent as the boat pulled into Ceres Harbour. The lights of the tavernas shone out across the water and the sound of music floated in the air. The evening magic was everywhere, but this time it failed to touch Pippa as she stepped carefully ashore.

* * *

The darkened, empty hospital corridor echoed with the sound of their footsteps as Pippa and Adonis hurried towards the private room in the medical unit where Nick Seferis was being cared for. Pippa had thrown on the spare uniform she always kept in her room and Adonis had slipped into a white coat, slinging his stethoscope around his neck.

Jim Burke's face registered relief as they entered the darkened room.

'He's very hot,' he whispered. 'A hundred and four degrees when we last checked.'

Pippa looked across at the medical sister; Jean Granby was an efficient young woman from Australia with a wide experience of nursing in the Far East.

'We'd better sponge Dr Seferis down to try and reduce the temperature, Sister Granby,' Pippa said.

The medical sister nodded. 'We've already sponged him an hour ago, but we'll repeat the procedure.'

'Give me a few minutes to make a full examination, Sister,' Adonis said as he settled himself on the side of the bed. He looked up at Pippa. 'I'll need an inspection trolley.'

Sister Granby motioned to her staff nurse, who wheeled up the necessary instruments.

'Nick, can you hear what I'm saying?' Adonis began, but after several seconds it was obvious that his colleague was semi-comatosed.

'I'm going to take some blood for microscopic examination, which should help the diagnosis,' Adonis said quietly. 'But I think we should start quinine treatment on the assumption that it's malaria. We'll have to inject the quinine now that Nick isn't capable of swallowing.'

As Adonis took the blood from Nick's arm, Pippa

noticed that their patient had begun to sweat profusely.

'I think Dr Seferis is going into the third stage,' she observed quietly.

Sister Granby nodded. 'Hopefully this may last only two or three hours after which the temperature should drop for a while. The malarial patients I've nursed usually had an interval of twenty-four to seventy-two hours before the symptoms returned again.'

'It's a relief that you're experienced in tropical nursing, Sister Granby,' Pippa said.

Sister Granby nodded. 'Don't worry, Sister Manson. Dr Seferis is in good hands. I'm going to stay on tonight to special him. I'm just back from a couple of days off, so I'm not tired.'

'I'll stay on if you like, Sister,' Pippa said.

'I'm sure there's no need,' Adonis said evenly. 'Sister Granby is coping admirably. You've had a long day, Sister Manson.'

That was certainly true, Pippa realised, as she felt the weariness creeping over her. There were plenty of night staff, and Sister Granby was an expert in tropical medicine, so Pippa could go away with a clear conscience. . .and from the stern look on Adonis's face she could see that he would disapprove if she stayed on in her wearied condition.

'I'll go and persuade the path lab technician to analyse this blood sample,' Adonis said. 'I'll come back about midnight, Dr Burke. But give me a call if you're worried.'

Jim Burke nodded. 'Sorry to drag you back from your evening off duty. But I thought you should know what was going on. And I didn't want to be technically in charge of the hospital without your permission, sir.'

'You were quite right to call me back, Jim,' Adonis told the young doctor. 'And you did a great job in my absence.'

Pippa saw the look of relief on Jim Burke's face. 'Well, if you don't need me I'll go off duty,' she said quietly. 'Goodnight, everyone.'

She sensed that Adonis would follow her. As she reached the door, he put out his arm and opened it for her.

'Is Nick going to be all right?' she asked quietly.

Adonis drew in his breath. 'I hope so. This is one of the diseases where the treatment hasn't advanced much since it was first diagnosed. But while the treatment has remained relatively static, the clever little mosquitoes have become more resistant. The best form of treatment is preventative: anti-malarial pills for several weeks before visiting and, during a stay in the Far East, mosquito nets, insecticide-spraying of dangerous areas to eliminate the pests, and covering all exposed skin between sunset and sunrise. But it's a bit late for that where Nick is concerned. We'll have to continue the quinine treatment and alleviate the febrile symptoms as they arise.'

They stopped off at the tiny path lab near the main entrance to the hospital. A dim light was burning beside the main desk, and Sotiris, the young technician who worked part-time, was waiting for the blood sample, having been summoned from his bed by a concerned Dr Burke.

'I should be able to isolate the malarial parasite, if it's present, in a few hours, sir,' Sotiris said.

'Let me know the minute you've found something,' Adonis said. He turned and looked down at Pippa. 'You really should go and rest now, Sister.'

'Goodnight, Dr Patras.' Pippa felt like a child who'd been reprimanded and sent to bed as she headed off towards the medical residents' quarters. Adonis seemed obsessed with the fact that his staff should be in good health. She wondered fleetingly if he'd had a bad experience because of an unhealthy member of staff. That might account for his unflinching stance. Whatever it was, it wasn't making her situation any easier. And just when she thought she was getting to know him as a man. . . Who knew what might have happened if they'd stayed out there in the moonlight?

The moonlight was now flooding the courtyard as she left the door from the hospital. She stopped in the middle of the courtyard and looked up at the starry sky. There was no shooting star tonight. . .no star on which to make her impossible wish.

She opened the door of her room and went in to find it had been cleaned and the cleaner had put fresh flowers in a vase beside the bed. The smell of the wild roses was welcoming and inviting. She'd come to love this little room; it was a haven, a retreat from the outside world.

Occasionally when she was off duty she went over and stayed at the Capodistrias house, but she found she had to make the effort to be sociable, which wasn't always easy at the end of a long day in hospital. Old Dr Demetrius was a kind host, but avid for information about what was going on at the hospital. So her visits to Symborio had become something of a duty.

She walked across her little room and lay down on the bed, peeling off her crumpled shirt and trousers. The friendly moon was shining in through the window and for a few minutes she lay basking in its rays, unwilling to light her bedside lamp and shatter the

magic of the moonlight. She allowed her thoughts to
return to the idyllic bay, where they'd stood looking
out across the sea. . .the feel of Adonis's arm around
her shoulder. . .and then his lips on hers. Had it meant
anything to him? Sadly she came to the conclusion that
his cold, harsh, totally professional manner since leaving the bay seemed to indicate that he'd forgotten the
whole incident.

CHAPTER EIGHT

THE heat of the Greek summer increased during July, and August was unbearable in the areas of the hospital where there was no air-conditioning. Pippa arranged for a shipment of large electric fans to be sent over from Rhodes, which helped to alleviate the problem. Apparently, it was the hottest summer for many years, and Pippa had to learn how to cope with it.

She also had to learn how to cope with her feelings for Adonis. But on a hot August morning, during a chance conversation with Sister Stangos, her secret hopes were again shattered.

Pippa was sitting by the open window, feeding one of the babies in the obstetric unit. One of the ways in which she kept in touch with all the different medical, surgical, orthopaedic and obstetric units was to spend some time actually working in them. At first she sensed a certain resentment from the sisters and staff nurses in charge of the units, because they assumed she was checking up on them. But as the weeks went by and the nursing staff realised that Pippa wasn't spying on them or looking to criticise their work, but simply working to ensure the smooth running of the hospital, they relaxed and took Pippa into their confidence. Medical and staffing problems were ironed out as soon as they arose, rather than being allowed to build up into niggling grudges against the administration.

One of Pippa's favourite nursing duties was to help out in Obstetrics with the baby feeds. The dear little week-old boy whom she was now feeding was sucking well, so Pippa took her eyes from him for a few seconds and looked out through the open window.

Down in the harbour she could see Adonis climbing aboard his boat, giving instructions to one of the crew members. Her heart started pounding.

He hadn't asked her to go out in the boat since that last trip to Ayias Emilianos, way back in June. To be honest, both she and Adonis had been exceptionally busy for the past few weeks, but she'd hoped that Adonis would have found time to repeat his invitation. The rapport of that afternoon had been so cruelly shattered, and ever since they'd remained, on the surface, merely professional colleagues. But when they met Pippa sensed, in a look or an apparently accidental touch of the hand, that Adonis remembered their feeling of closeness, and she tried to convince herself that it was because they were both so busy that their relationship hadn't progressed.

Nick Seferis was recovering slowly from his malaria, but was unlikely to take up hospital duties for several weeks, so Adonis had been spending all his waking hours in the hospital, and the prospect of another barbecue seemed remote.

'I wonder where Dr Patras is off to.'

Pippa looked up at the sound of Ariadne's voice. Her colleague was standing behind her, a disposable nappy in one hand and a feeding bottle in the other.

'I've no idea,' Pippa replied lightly, turning her attention back to the baby boy in her arms.

'Surely Dr Patras tells you when he's leaving the hospital,' Ariadne persisted. 'I mean, you share the responsibility between you.'

Pippa bridled, sensing that Ariadne was fishing

again. 'Dr Patras tells me when he's leaving the hospital, but I never ask where he's going. He leaves instructions with Reception so that they can call him if necessary.'

Pippa glanced around her. There were no mothers in the nursery that morning, which was a pity. This meant that Ariadne would start up her questioning again, and lately Pippa had come to resent the intrusion. In the first weeks of her time here on Ceres Pippa had valued Ariadne's friendship, but recently the questioning had become too intense. She wanted to be left alone to sort out her emotional tangle.

Ariadne moved to pick up the baby in the cot next to the one beside Pippa. As soon as the baby was sucking on the bottle, Ariadne turned her attention on Pippa again.

'Do I sense a cooling down in your relationship with Adonis?'

Pippa took a deep breath to calm herself. Ariadne's interest in her personal life was becoming obsessive. Over the past few weeks Pippa had made a tremendous effort to conceal her feelings for Adonis from the rest of the hospital staff. Since his revelation that the betrothal was a sham, both for him and for Cassiopi, she'd allowed herself to harbour hopes that they might eventually have a future together, but she'd taken great pains to keep the secret that Adonis had confided to her.

'With respect, Ariadne, I don't think that's any of your business,' Pippa said quietly.

The baby had finished feeding. Pippa put the bottle down on the cotside table and held him against her, gently rubbing his back.

'There, there, little one,' she murmured, studiously

ignoring the gasp of indignation from her colleague.
'Let's have a little burp, shall we?'

'My only concern is for you, Pippa,' Ariadne
retorted. 'I hope your affair is cooling down, because
when Cassiopi comes back from America——'

'Cassiopi has no hold on Adonis!' Pippa's words
were blurted out before she had time to consider the
consequences.

Ariadne's eyes narrowed. 'Whatever gave you that
idea? I suppose Adonis has been feeding you some
clever story about the betrothal being a sham. That
man will go to any lengths to have his cake and eat it.'

Pippa felt her heart go cold with fear. Ariadne had
known Adonis so much longer than she. They had
grown up together. Was it possible that Pippa's worst
fears were true. . .that Adonis had duped her with a
story that was untrue? Was that why he'd told her that
it was in the strictest confidence and she must tell no
one? But she mustn't admit her fears to Ariadne.

Silently she rubbed the baby's back until he expelled
some air. His eyes had closed and she put him back in
his cot by the window. Briefly she noticed that
Adonis's boat was leaving the harbour now, but he
must have gone below, because only the crew were
visible.

'My only concern is for you, Pippa,' Ariadne
repeated quietly. 'And I'm warning you that if
Adonis——'

'And I'm warning you, Ariadne,' Pippa interrupted
tersely. 'Stay out of my personal life. I was grateful for
your help when I arrived here as a newcomer but now
I find your questioning is becoming intrusive. My
personal life has nothing to do with my professional
life and I'll thank you to——'

She broke off in mid-sentence. Adonis was walking through the open door, striding towards her.

'I thought you were on your boat,' she finished lamely.

Adonis smiled. 'Watching from the window, were you? Every move I make is monitored by someone. I was simply instructing the crew, who are collecting some supplies for me.'

He glanced across at Ariadne, who was looking decidedly uncomfortable. 'I couldn't help overhearing what Sister Manson was saying and I couldn't agree more. Philippa's private life has nothing to do with you, Ariadne, so please keep your pretty little nose out of it.'

Pippa could see the anger boiling beneath Ariadne's calm exterior, but, to her colleague's credit, she didn't voice any of it.

'Is this a professional call, Dr Patras?' Ariadne asked in an icy voice.

'Yes, it is. I've come to ask Sister Manson to accompany me over to Orthopaedics, where we're about to organise a wedding.'

Ariadne's eyes widened, but she remained silent.

'Gina and Geoffrey, two of our patients, are to be married next week,' Adonis continued, obviously enjoying Ariadne's discomfiture. 'Would you like to come, Sister Stangos?'

'If my duties permit, Dr Patras,' Ariadne replied coldly.

Pippa pulled up the side of the cot and left the sleeping baby, walking determinedly towards the door.

She paused on the threshold. 'Unless there is a staff shortage, Sister Stangos, I may not be available for help with the baby feeds,' she said quietly, feeling the

sadness that this decision would cause her. She loved
feeding the babies, but she would have to forgo this if
she was to be grilled and emotionally upset every time
she came in contact with Ariadne Stangos.

Ariadne looked up. 'Then you'd better replace
Nurse Chrisanthe, because her work record is abysmal.
She comes in when she feels like it and takes days off
without so much as a by-your-leave. I need another
nurse I can rely on.'

'I've sent a note to Nurse Chrisanthe, asking her to
come and see me again,' Pippa replied evenly. 'I saw
her once, soon after I came here, but the interview
was inconclusive. She promised to be more reliable,
but obviously——'

'You'd better make sure there's nothing wrong with
her health,' Adonis broke in warningly. 'She can't
work if she's ill.'

Pippa nodded. 'I'll check on that as soon as
Chrisanthe returns. In the meantime, I'll assign
another nurse to Obstetrics.'

Ariadne nodded but didn't look up. 'Thank you,
Sister.'

Pippa walked off down the corridor. 'Oh, it's all so
infuriating!' she blurted out as Adonis joined her and
they walked on together. 'I can't bear hard feelings
between any of the staff and myself. I was getting on
so well with Ariadne, but she tries my patience to
the limit. I've asked her not to pry into my affairs,
but——'

'I warned you not to confide in her when you first
came here,' Adonis said slowly.

'Yes, you did. . .and I should have listened. But I
needed someone to confide in. I didn't know she would
persist in interrogating me like this. I mean. . .'

She paused, and turned to look up at Adonis. His enigmatic eyes gave her no clue as to how he was feeling.

'I suppose she told you not to trust me, is that it, Pippa?' Adonis asked.

Pippa nodded, unable to put her thoughts into words.

'Then it's her word against mine,' he said with icy calm. 'Whom will you believe?'

She turned away. 'I don't know what to believe any more. I'd like to believe you, Adonis. . . I really would, but it seems such an incredible story. I mean ——'

The sentence was never finished. Sister Diana Demotis had pushed open the doors of the orthopaedic unit and was smiling across at them. 'Ah, there you are, Dr Patras. Gina and Geoffrey were hoping you would arrive soon. And Sister Manson too. At last we can get the wedding arrangements finalised. Do come this way.'

Pippa followed Adonis into the orthopaedic unit.

For the next few minutes she somehow managed to put on a cheerful act as they organised the wedding preparations, gathered around Geoffrey's bedside.

Gina was sitting on a chair, holding Geoffrey's hand and smiling throughout the proceedings.

'I can't wait for our wedding-day,' she was saying happily. 'You should see how lovely I've made our little flat, Geoffrey. And I've been over to Rhodes and bought a fabulous dress, nice and full and loose enough to cover my bulge. I'm not going to show it to you before the actual day, because it would bring bad luck. It's a pity you're still stuck in this traction. How much longer will Geoffrey be stuck here, Doctor?'

Adonis was holding up the latest X-rays to the light. 'Perhaps another month. The time it takes to heal bones is difficult to predict. But this seems to be going on well. I hope Geoffrey will be able to join you in the flat before the baby's born.'

'Have you fixed which priest will come?' Sister Demotis asked.

'Yes, the English chapel minister who retired to live in Epano will be most happy to perform the ceremony,' Pippa replied, remembering the long session she'd had with the worthy man, who was not altogether sure what would be required of him, but was anxious to help the young couple in any way he could.

'And the wedding feast?' Diana Demotis persisted. 'We must have a good spread.'

'I've arranged with the Olympic Hotel that they will organise the buffet. Dr Demetrius Capodistrias has insisted on paying the bill.'

Here again, Pippa was embroidering the truth. She hadn't known where the money would come from until she'd casually mentioned the wedding on one of her evenings in the Capodistrias house. She'd had to convince Dr Demetrius that Gina and Geoffrey were a couple worthy of his patronage, and she was hoping the bride and groom wouldn't let her down.

'Well, that seems to be all we need to settle at the moment,' Sister Demotis said happily. 'I think it's going to be a marvellous occasion for the hospital. Several people from the town have asked if they can come in for the afternoon, and of course I've had to say yes. My mother and father thought they would pop in just for a few minutes. And of course everyone will bring presents. I suggested something for Gina's and Geoffrey's flat and——'

'Thank you so much, Sister,' Pippa broke in. 'I can see you've got everything under control, so I'll leave you to it.'

Adonis followed her out into the corridor and as they walked together Pippa was intensely aware of his fingers almost touching her own.

'The plans seem to be working out,' she began tentatively.

'Yes; I don't think we need to worry any more,' he replied in a dead-pan tone.

Oh, God! How impersonal he sounds! Pippa thought. I've hurt him by refusing to believe in him. She looked up at the impassive face beside her.

'I'm going to take a couple of hours off this afternoon. I've got some shopping to do in Ceres Town,' she said, hoping he would speak to her again. . .say anything, but not ignore her like this.

'Take all the time you like. The hospital won't fall down without you.'

He strode away and left her in the middle of the corridor. A porter was passing, wheeling a patient to X-Ray.

'*Kalimera*, Sister. Good morning.'

'*Kalimera*,' Pippa replied automatically, desperately holding back the tears that threatened to break through. She hurried on to her own room and closed the door.

Elena, the medical secretary, was clearing away her things from the desk, gathering up case-notes and letters.

'Are you all right, Sister?' she asked in her gentle, highly accented voice.

Pippa tried to smile. 'Yes, I'm fine. I've got a bit of a headache, but it will pass.'

'Why don't you take the afternoon off, Sister?' the older woman asked. 'There's no need for you to work such long hours in this heat. In Greece we take things easier than you do in your country. Why don't you go out on the water in a boat where it is cool? I am sure Dr Patras would be delighted to take you. The last time you went out together——'

'I'm sure Dr Patras has better things to do,' Pippa broke in tersely, thinking that her efforts to conceal her feelings for Adonis had been useless where the hospital staff were concerned. 'But I will go out this afternoon. I'll take the rest of the day off unless I get an emergency call.'

'I'll try to ensure that you don't,' the kindly secretary said. 'I think you need a rest, Sister. You shouldn't work so hard in this climate.'

'I love my work here, Elena, so please don't worry about me,' Pippa said quietly.

Pippa walked along the harbourside, pausing to look around the sponge shop. Yes, she assured the shop-keeper, she was going to buy sponges for her family when she returned to England; one for her mother, another for her father. . . Would Simon and Peter appreciate sponges? Probably not. She would come back another day when she'd made up her mind.

She walked out into the hot afternoon sun. It was so difficult to make decisions in this sweltering heat. Funny how her thoughts were actually turning towards home again. She was more than halfway through her contract. Decisions would have to be made soon. . .

and far more important decisions than how many sponges to buy.

'Oh, Sister Manson, thank God I've found you!'

A young Greek sailor was plucking at her elbow, staring into her face with an alarming expression. He was only marginally taller than she was, but he was of a stocky build, his bare arms covered in tattoo marks.

'Do I know you?'

'I'm Giorgios, Chrisanthe's husband.'

'Ah; we were discussing Chrisanthe this morning. I wonder——'

'Sister, you have to come with me now. There is no time to lose. I was on my way to the hospital and my wife told me to see you. . .no one else. She trusts you and. . .follow me, please.'

Giorgio was pulling on her arm. She had to go with him.

The afternoon sun beat down on the already hot stones of the *kali strata*, the uneven, cobble-stoned track that ran from the lower town of Kato to the upper town of Epano. Underfoot, the stones were organised into steps. Pippa had already counted more than a hundred before she paused at a bend in the track to catch her breath.

She couldn't believe that she was actually running up this incredibly steep track! For the last few weeks she'd been exercising her injured foot as much as possible, getting up early to practise walking up and down the steps down to the harbour before anyone was around to watch her. And her efforts had paid off. The foot had strengthened; she was sure the bone was thickening. She was almost one hundred per cent fit again and the joy at her new-found strength was only tinged with apprehension at what she might find at

Chrisanthe's house. The urgency of the situation spurred her on.

Looking out between a gap in the houses, she could see the blue expanse of the bay; there wasn't a breath of air to waft across the boats in the harbour and there seemed to be no activity. Most people were taking a siesta, waiting out the hours before sundown.

Chrisanthe's house couldn't be much further. Both feet were beginning to ache now but she kept going, matching her speed to that of the young man beside her. She breathed a sigh of relief when he stopped at a house with blue shutters and pushed open a door.

Pippa stepped into the relative cool of the small living-room. The ancient thick walls helped to hold out the sun's heat. The room was simply furnished with wooden furniture. Several cushions scattered over the chairs and the narrow settee helped to soften the stark simplicity. A vase of fresh lilies on the square table scented the air.

The young man turned around. 'You must be kind to my wife. Chrisanthe told me you had called her into your office to discipline her.'

'Please, Giorgios, you must understand the situation. I have to ensure the smooth running of the hospital and if one of my nurses is persistently absent then I have to find out why. When I asked Chrisanthe to come and see me she explained that she'd taken on extra work looking after her mother, but she would ask her sisters to release her from her daily commitment and then she would never have to be absent.'

Giorgios motioned for Pippa to sit down on one of the wooden chairs beside the table. Slowly he sank down opposite, moving the flowers so that he could look Pippa full in the face.

'Is that what Chrisanthe told you?'

Pippa nodded. 'I was sorry to hear that Chrisanthe had so many family commitments but when a nurse is employed in a professional capacity——'

'Chrisanthe's mother has been dead for over ten years and she has no sisters, only a couple of brothers who live in Rhodes with her father. We are quite alone on this little island, because the family didn't want us to marry. They don't like the idea of my travelling the world without my wife. But I plan to save enough to buy a little shop here and then we will be together all the time.'

'But if Chrisanthe has no mother or sisters, what is taking up her time?' Pippa asked in a firm but gentle voice.

The young husband hesitated, running a dark, weather-beaten hand through his long black hair.

'She thinks she is going to have a baby. . . We are both longing for a child. But for the past three months, since she first thought a child was on the way, she has been ill. She's sick every morning, and sometimes during the day.'

'But why didn't she tell me this?'

'Because she was afraid she would lose her job. She's only been at the hospital for a few months and we need the money. She was taken on as an auxiliary nurse, to work under supervision, but she has no nursing qualifications. She thought if she could conceal the pregnancy for as long as possible you would take her back after the baby is born. But now I don't think there will be any baby.'

Pippa felt a cold shiver down her spine as she heard the young man's desolate voice. 'Why do you say that?' she asked gently.

The young man gave a deep sigh. 'I arrived back this morning. My ship is anchored at Rhodes for a few days. I took the ferry here and found Chrisanthe in bed. She says she's no longer pregnant.'

'I must see her at once.' Pippa jumped to her feet. 'She obviously needs help.'

The young man hurried ahead.

'Come through to the bedroom, Sister.'

Pippa went through to the back of the house. The bedroom was built into the sheer rock of the hillside. Only a tiny window carved out of the top of the bedroom wall gave a glimpse of the strong sunlight that flooded the small back garden.

Chrisanthe lay very still in the white-counterpaned bed. Her eyes were closed and only the flickering of her eyelashes indicated that she was awake.

'Chrisanthe, I've come to help you,' Pippa began as she sat down on the edge of the bed and reached across to take hold of the young woman's hand. Oh, my God, she's so hot. . . She's feverish! Pippa felt for Chrisanthe's pulse at the wrist. It was far too rapid.

'I've lost my baby, Sister,' Chrisanthe said tonelessly. 'I'm bleeding.'

'Chrisanthe, have you —— ?'

'No, I haven't done anything to myself. I wanted this baby.'

'I'm going to examine you, Chrisanthe,' Pippa said gently.

The young woman shrugged. 'If you like. But it won't do any good.'

Giorgios had already gone back into the livingroom. Pippa pulled back the covers and gently palpated the abdomen. As her practised fingers touched the region of the right iliac fossa Chrisanthe cried out.

'Oh, please, not there, don't touch me there, Sister. It hurts so badly.'

Pippa was rapidly trying to form a diagnosis as she continued her examination. The pain in the right iliac fossa could indicate appendicitis, but, on the other hand, she had to consider the other symptoms: amenorrhoea — Chrysanthe's periods had been absent for three months — vaginal bleeding for several hours, coupled with the rapid pulse and high temperature.

It might be an ectopic pregnancy in one of the fallopian tubes, in which case, Chrisanthe must be hospitalised at once so that an emergency laparoscopy could be performed. If this revealed an ectopic pregnancy, then a laparotomy would have to be performed to ligate the bleeding points and remove the affected tube.

'I'm going to take you into the hospital, Chrisanthe,' Pippa said gently. 'You're going to need some treatment.'

Chrisanthe's eyes widened. 'But I can't walk, Sister. And the ambulance can't get up the *kali strata*.'

'The ambulance can drive up the new road to reach the top of the *kali strata*,' Pippa assured her. 'And we can carry you by stretcher to that point.'

She moved quickly through into the living-room, instructing Giorgios to hurry to the hospital with her hastily scribbled note.

It was actually only ten minutes, but it seemed like an eternity until Pippa heard the welcome sound of the ambulance siren tearing up the new road. Moments later she heard the sound of feet running down the steps of the *kali strata* and Adonis, followed by a couple of porters with a stretcher, burst into the tiny house.

'I came as quickly as I could.' Adonis looked down at Pippa with quizzical eyes. 'Are you OK?'

'I'm fine,' she said briefly. 'But I think Chrisanthe may have an ectopic. We'll have to operate at once.'

As the ambulance tore down the new road Adonis was already fixing an intravenous infusion of glucose and saline into Chrisanthe's arm.

'We'll do grouping and cross-matching as soon as we get to hospital,' he said quietly to Pippa as she fixed Chrisanthe's arm on to a splint. 'She's going to need some blood as soon as possible.'

Pippa looked down at her patient. 'Chrisanthe. . . Chrisanthe,' she repeated, but the young woman had lost consciousness.

The young husband still clasped her hand in his. 'Is she going to be all right, Sister?'

'We'll do everything we possibly can,' Pippa said. 'The speed with which we can start this operation is most important.' She couldn't be over-optimistic simply to allay the young husband's fears. He had to know the truth even if it hurt.

'It's a good thing you ran up the *kali strata* with me just now,' Giorgios said quietly. 'If you hadn't been so quick it might have been too late.'

'You ran up the *kali strata*?' Adonis repeated, momentarily glancing down at Pippa's feet. She'd slipped off her shoes to ease the aching feeling. She was sure he would disapprove, but when their eyes met she saw nothing but admiration. And she saw something else, she could see her own concern mirrored in his eyes as she prayed that they would be in time to save Chrisanthe's life.

CHAPTER NINE

THE small operating-theatre had been prepared and the surgical team were waiting for Adonis and Pippa. Pippa turned to look at Adonis as she slipped her fingers into the sterile gloves which one of the theatre nurses was holding out for her.

'Do you agree with my diagnosis?' she asked.

'In principle,' was his guarded reply. 'Certainly when I did an internal examination a few minutes ago our patient had extreme tenderness in the area over the gravid tube and in the pouch of Douglas. It would seem that there could be a tubal pregnancy, but we mustn't jump to conclusions until we've seen what the laparoscopy will show us.'

Adonis approached the table. Pippa handed him a scalpel so that a small incision in the skin could be prepared.

'Diagnosis confirmed, Sister,' Adonis muttered tersely as the obvious signs of a tubal pregnancy showed up. 'The fallopian tube has ruptured, so I'm going to ligate the bleeding points and remove the affected tube. We'll need to open this up a bit further. . .'

The intricate operation continued amid a tense atmosphere. It wasn't just the fact that they were operating on a colleague that gave the team this sense of urgency. It was also the gnawing fear that the patient wouldn't pull through her ordeal. Chrisanthe had lost a lot of blood and was in deep shock before

the commencement of the operation, and there had
been bleeding into the peritoneum, bringing with it
the danger of infection and abdominal complications.

Even Jim Burke, the usually cheerful young
Australian doctor; was showing signs of anxiety as he
checked his anaesthesia equipment.

'She's a poor colour, sir,' he announced tentatively.

'So would you be if you were bleeding everywhere,'
Adonis replied evenly.

Jim Burke leaned forward. 'How much longer will it
take to —— ?'

'I'm working as quickly as I can, Jim! Stop
panicking!'

'Sorry, sir.'

Pippa glanced up at Adonis, but the eyes above the
mask gave no indication of his fears. She felt a strange
shiver running through her as their eyes met. She knew
then that she didn't know this man at all. He was a
complete enigma, a stranger who had walked into her
life and captivated her. But, in the same manner, he
could just as easily walk straight out again and leave
her with a feeling of utter desolation.

Determinedly, she brought her thoughts back to the
task in hand. They had to save this young woman's life
if it was humanly possible. And Adonis was one of the
best surgeons she'd ever assisted. If he couldn't save
the patient, then no one else could.

A couple of hours had passed before Adonis pulled
himself to his full height and he peeled off his gloves
and glanced around the assembled surgical team.

'She'll pull through if we make a combined effort.
Thanks for your help so far, but the treatment has only
just begun. The drainage tubes will help to clear up

the abdomen, but the nursing staff must monitor every small change in pulse-rate and report directly to me.'

He strode off to the changing-room at the side of the theatre. Pippa accompanied their patient through into Recovery. Ariadne Stangos, in her capacity as sister in charge of Obstetrics and Gynaecology, was waiting for her patient, an anxious expression on her face.

'I'll take over here, Sister,' she said quietly to Pippa. 'Chrisanthe will be coming back to the gynae unit. What are the instructions for her post-operative care?'

Pippa quickly briefed her colleague. The petty squabbling of the morning was a thing of the past now that they were both involved in an emergency.

'Let me know as soon as Chrisanthe comes round,' Pippa said. 'She's going to need a great deal of moral support over the question of losing this baby. The remaining tube appears to be healthy, as far as I could make out, so she could become pregnant again in the future. The possibility of being a mother should not be ruled out.' She turned away. 'I'll be in my room if you need me.'

Ariadne stretched out her hand towards Pippa and touched her lightly on the arm.

'Thank you, Sister, and thanks for the extra nursing staff you sent me. I've got a good, experienced team assembled to care for Chrisanthe.' For a few seconds she looked away before adding, 'I didn't mean to pry into your affairs. My only concern——'

'Thanks, Ariadne. Let's leave it, shall we?' Pippa replied lightly, making an attempt at an impersonal smile.

'But we can still be friends, I hope,' Ariadne persisted.

Pippa took a deep breath. 'Of course. . .so long
as ——'

'So long as I don't interfere in your private life.
Point taken.'

'Keep an eye on the IV,' Pippa said, briskly changing the subject. 'It will need changing shortly. There's
some more blood just coming up to body temperature.
And there must be constant monitoring of temperature, pulse, respiration, blood-pressure, drainage
tubes. Let me know immediately if there's any fall in
the blood-pressure.'

Pippa began to check on the latest readings. Gently
she eased the airway out of her patient's mouth and
listened to the stertorous breathing.

'Please, God, let her pull through,' she murmured
under her breath.

A week passed before Adonis declared that Chrisanthe
was out of danger. The entire staff of the hospital
breathed a sigh of relief. It was as if they had been
experiencing a period of mourning which had now
been lifted.

'The wedding can go ahead as planned,' Pippa told
the delighted Demotis on her morning round of Orthopaedics. They had been holding off the celebrations
until Adonis could assure them that Chrisanthe was
recovering.

Two days later, on the morning of the wedding, Sister
Demotis got her nurses to fill every available vase with
flowers. The windows were wide open and the priest
at the nearby church had arranged for the bells to be
rung before the wedding ceremony took place in the
hospital.

The retired minister, who had come to Ceres hoping for some peace and quiet, rose to the occasion and beamed around at the assembled throng in the orthopaedic unit.

The service was in English, so half of the Greek guests, invited and uninvited, couldn't understand a word of it, but everyone was obviously enjoying themselves.

The secret of Gina's dress was revealed. It was a pale pink chiffon creation and flowed from the shoulders to the floor. She wore an attractive pink floral head-dress and looked radiant as Geoffrey leaned across his traction to slip the gold band on her finger.

'With this ring I thee. . .'

Pippa looked around the orthopaedic unit. There was hardly a dry eye in the room. And then she saw Adonis, standing by the door. Their eyes met briefly before he looked away.

She felt the now familiar pain in the pit of her stomach. Since the morning that Ariadne had questioned Pippa's trust in Adonis, there had only been brief encounters in the hospital, and then purely professional. She remembered the hurt expression in Adonis's eyes when he'd asked who she believed was telling the truth.

She turned back to look at the bride and groom, who were enjoying the first kiss of their marriage, watched over by an adoring crowd.

'Ah, don't they look lovely?' Sister Demotis cried. 'Come along, nurses, hand the glasses of champagne around. Here's to the happy couple!'

The glasses were raised in a toast, and now it was Gina's turn to start weeping. 'It's all so wonderful,' she murmured through the tears. 'Like the end of a fairy-tale.'

Pippa smiled. 'It's only the beginning, Gina. The best is yet to come.'

'Oh, I hope so, Sister,' Gina whispered. 'I mean, I'm still scared about having the baby, but——'

'There's no need to be scared,' Adonis put in, as he moved quietly to the bride's side. 'You'll be in good hands when your time comes. Sister Manson and I will be around to see that there are no problems.'

Pippa glanced shyly at Adonis. He still had the infuriating way of setting her pulses racing whenever he was near her. How was she ever to get this man out of her life? But did she want him out of her life?

'I have to go up to the detox unit this afternoon, Sister,' Adonis was saying to her in an even, professional voice. 'I know you wanted to see round it, so if you would like to come with me I'll ask Dr Samos if this would be convenient.'

Pippa hesitated. 'I would like that very much, Dr Patras.' She glanced around her, but no one was interested in their conversation. 'Are you holding out the olive-branch, Adonis?' she asked under her breath.

He gave her a deliciously wicked and thoroughly unprofessional smile. 'Perhaps.'

Sister Demotis was approaching from the other side of the ward, carrying a bottle of champagne. 'Dr Patras, would you do the honours, please?'

'Certainly, Sister,' Adonis replied as he began to peel off the foil wrapping from the cork.

Under cover of the noise made by the popping of the cork, Adonis told Pippa, 'I haven't seen much of you lately. Where have you been?'

'I've been here all the time,' she muttered, before smiling and raising her glass towards him.

Adonis chinked his glass against hers. 'Let's leave as soon as we can,' he replied briskly.

Pippa nodded, but moved away to help Sister Demotis with the socialising, ensuring that everyone was enjoying themselves and having enough to eat and drink. As soon as the buffet was over, they started to clear away the plates.

The smoked salmon, prawns, chicken, lobster and salad served with crusty Greek bread and green olives had been excellent, and Pippa congratulated the staff, who had come from the Olympic Hotel down in the harbour, explaining to the head waiter that Dr Capodistrias would settle the account.

Gina remained beside her new husband, holding his hand and looking adoringly into his eyes.

'If only you could take this contraption off for a couple of hours,' Geoffrey said to Adonis. 'Couldn't you just turn the other way for a little while?'

Adonis smiled. 'Sorry, Geoffrey. You wouldn't like it if your leg collapsed and put you back a few months. I know it's rotten luck on your wedding-day, but you'll have to be patient.'

'A few more weeks and then you can move into your little love nest,' Pippa added, gently patting Geoffrey's hand.

'I've got to check on Chrisanthe,' Adonis told Pippa as they walked out of the orthopaedic unit and down the corridor.

'I'll come with you,' Pippa said. 'I haven't seen her today, but I know Ariadne and her staff are doing an excellent job.'

She felt Adonis stiffen by her side at the mention of

Ariadne's name. 'Professional matters only today
when you see Ariadne, Philippa.'

'Of course. Ariadne and I have agreed to restrict
our friendship to hospital matters. . .for the moment,
until. . .until we've got over our difference of opinion.'

'So there is a difference of opinion?' he persisted.
'Do I take it you're having second thoughts about what
Ariadne told you?'

She took a deep breath. 'Let's say I'm keeping an
open mind on the subject.'

She felt his hand stealing under her elbow, that firm,
sensual touch which always excited her. 'And about
time too!' he said, his fingers squeezing her arm.

Chrisanthe was propped up on her pillows. The
drainage tubes had been removed and she was now
free to sit out of bed, but she remained most of the
day lying down, since she still felt very weak.

'What are my chances of another baby, Doctor?'
she asked after Adonis had examined her.

He hesitated. 'I would say fifty-fifty, Chrisanthe.
You've still got one healthy fallopian tube left. So it is
possible.'

Chrisanthe sighed. 'I hope so. . .' She paused before
continuing in her slow, breathless voice, 'Thank you
so much for everything. I'm sorry I gave you so much
trouble, Sister. I would have told you about the
pregnancy before, but I wasn't really sure myself. It
never did feel like a normal pregnancy. And then I
didn't want to lose my job.'

'There's no fear of that, Chrisanthe,' Pippa assured
her. 'I'll see to it that your job is held open for you
until you're fit enough to return.'

'You can rely on Sister Manson to see to it person-

ally,' Ariadne put in as she approached the bed from
the other side of the unit.

Pippa smiled at her colleague, although she was
taken aback by Ariadne's continued attempt to curry
favour with her. There was something a little too
saccharine about the compliments that flowed during
professional hours. The situation was false; she would
prefer Ariadne to let her hair down and say what she
really thought.

The afternoon sun beat down mercilessly as the Land
Rover climbed the hot, concrete-surfaced road. Pippa
eased herself gently around the passenger seat beside
Adonis.

'What time is Dr Samos expecting us?' she asked
him.

His hands tightened on the wheel as he negotiated a
particularly difficult bend.

'About seven,' he replied evenly.

'Seven? But it's barely three o'clock. I thought you
said. . .'

He smiled and for a brief moment took his eyes
from the road. 'I merely said I would ask Dr Samos
when it was convenient to look around. When I
phoned he said seven would be perfect.'

'You mean you suggested seven?'

Adonis laughed, a deep, virile, masculine sound that
sent shivers of anticipation tinged with apprehension
down Pippa's spine.

'I didn't want to jeopardise our visit by making it in
the heat of the afternoon.'

And meanwhile. . .?'

'Meanwhile we'll join up with the crew of the boat
over in the next bay and spend the afternoon out on

the water, where it's much cooler. I thought it better
to embark over here, far from prying eyes.'

'Adonis, you're impossible! You'll go to any lengths
to. . .' She broke off, suddenly aware that she was
repeating some of Ariadne's words. Her colleague had
insisted that Adonis would go to any lengths to have
his cake and eat it.

Desperately she tried to quell the feelings of misgiv-
ing. She'd told Adonis she was keeping an open mind,
and that was what she must do. . .at least for the next
few hours. It would be a pity to spoil their afternoon
of reconciliation.

'You were saying, Philippa?' Adonis persisted.
'What lengths will I go to?'

'I was merely observing that you like to have your
own way,' Pippa began cautiously.

'And why not? When I know what I want I go for
it.'

He had taken one hand from the wheel to cover her
own. They were hurtling over the stony track on the
other side of the hill. Pippa closed her eyes.

'Adonis. . . I have to say that——'

'Leave it, Pippa. . .until we can relax and get to
know each other again. It was a difference of opinion.
But we've got all afternoon to sort it out. . .'

CHAPTER TEN

As ADONIS drove down the steep hill Pippa could see the blue water of the sea gently rippling in the wide bay and continuing out to the horizen, dotted with small sun-bedazzled green and brown islands.

'The crew are waiting down there,' Adonis said. 'They're a good team and very loyal. I can trust them implicitly. I know they would never relay any information about you and me.'

Pippa's heart started to beat faster. 'Why are you telling me this, Adonis?'

'Because I want you to relax this afternoon. I want you to feel free and uninhibited. You're much too tense. It's almost as if you're waiting for some emergency to happen. Remember, you have every right to take a few hours off from hospital. It will make you all the more efficient when you return.'

'It's not the work that makes me tense, Adonis,' Pippa said quietly. 'It's you and me together. . .alone.'

'I know,' he replied huskily. 'But you mustn't worry. No one knows we are here.'

She turned away and looked out across the sparse wilderness of the uninhabited valley. A dried-up riverbed cut through the gorge beside the road, which was now no more than a rocky track. They were quite alone; that was true. But this wasn't what was really worrying her. Adonis had completely misinterpreted her fear. Should she try to explain. . .and risk shattering their illusion of calm?

She glanced up at the strong profile outlined in the afternoon sunlight. Adonis looked so handsome. . . and so trustworthy. How could she continue to doubt his intentions towards her? She leaned back against the seat and deliberately silenced her nagging doubts.

He brought the Land Rover to a halt beside a tiny wooden jetty. One of his crew came running off the boat, hands outstretched to lift the bag that Adonis was removing from the boot.

Pippa followed Adonis on to the boat. Another crew member held out a tray of drinks towards her as soon as she was settled on deck beneath the striped canvas awning that protected them from the sun's rays.

As she drank the deliciously cold fruit juice she looked up at Adonis, who had settled himself beside her, one arm outstretched along the back of the wooden seat.

The boat was moving out to sea, leaving the harbour. Pippa leaned back and closed her eyes, revelling in the touch of Adonis's arm around her shoulders. For the next few hours she would pretend there was no tomorrow. . .only today.

They anchored off one of the small uninhabited islands and went ashore, leaving the crew to carry over the bags.

'I haven't brought my bikini,' Pippa said, glancing down at her uniform dress. 'I thought we were going on a professional visit to the detox unit.'

'No need for swimsuits on this desert isle,' Adonis said, as he reached for her hand and led her over the rocks to a tiny deserted cove.

It seemed so natural to peel off her clothes and follow Adonis into the deliciously cool water. Nudity had never been a problem to her. With two brothers in the house when she was small, she'd never considered that the naked body was something to avoid. And her nursing training had curbed any inhibitions she might have adopted as she'd grown up.

Her skin revelled in the cooling balm of the sea. Together they struck out away from shore, swimming side by side with strong, even strokes.

'Look over there, Pippa!' Adonis raised his arm and pointed towards some huge fish leaping high out of the water.

'Porpoises!' he cried excitedly.

Pippa could see the vivid illumination of the sun shining on their silvery scales as they jumped in a complete rainbow arc before diving back below the surface of the water.

'We're a long way from shore,' she said, turning over on to her back to rest on the surface of the water, hoping to gather her strength before the return swim.

She closed her eyes against the strong rays of the sun. It was a delicious feeling, the cool water at her back, the hot sun warming her front. And it was so much more sensuous because her skin was in direct contact with the elements.

'We're quite safe out here,' Adonis said. 'The salt of the sea is concentrated here and it would be difficult to drown. We can lie on the sea as if it's a mattress.'

She opened her eyes. He looked so relaxed as he lay beside her on their watery bed.

'I'd like to stay out here forever,' she murmured, half to herself.

Adonis gave her a long, slow, loving smile. 'And I'd like to stay here with you.'

They remained on the surface of the water for several moments of exquisite magic. Pippa felt as if they were two sea creatures, in their kingdom of the waves.

'We'll have to go back,' Pippa said gently. 'I hope I've got the strength to swim that far.'

'I can carry you along,' Adonis said huskily. 'Don't worry, I'm here beside you.'

And she didn't worry as they swam back through the water towards the shore.

The crew had placed towels and a hamper of food in their secret bay before going back to the boat.

'Unobtrusive and efficient, the crew.' Pippa smiled as she enveloped herself in a large white fluffy towel.

'You should always look like that,' Adonis said, striding towards her over the hot sand.

'Like what?'

'Like a young mermaid.' He kissed the tip of her nose. 'Come and have some food. I'm starving.'

They ate their picnic sitting on the soft white sand; ham, feta cheese, olives, crusty bread, fruit and cold white wine in the crystal glasses. Adonis had spread the picnic rug at the edge of the sea so that they could keep cool by dipping their toes in the bay.

He tossed some crumbs into the water and the fish swam to gobble greedily, their wild movements churning up the surface of the water in small waves.

Afterwards they lay back on the sand. Pippa looked up at the blue sky. Unconsciously, she pulled the towel around her and moved to one side.

'Are you afraid of me?' Adonis asked quietly.

She shook her head. 'I'm afraid of myself,' she murmured as she felt the stirrings of her passion for this highly sensuous, intensely desirable man. 'Whenever we're together I forget all our problems. I forget that —— '

His lips silenced her in a long, sensual kiss.

'And that's how it should be,' he whispered huskily, as he pulled away for a few moments to gaze down at her. 'There are no problems we can't handle together, Philippa. It's only a question of time. Please, let us play the waiting game, as you say.'

His hands moved gently to caress the skin at the nape of her neck. Then, gently, ever so gently, he slowly pulled the towel away from her breasts, his fingers tantalising as they teased her nipples. She arched her body towards him, her arms twining themselves around his neck to pull herself against him. His fingers slipped down the side of her thighs and she gave an involuntary moan. There was no going back now. The world had ceased to exist. They were two lovers in an immortal time span.

But even as her body flamed with passion Pippa became aware of voices from the other side of the small island. She felt Adonis tense as he pulled himself away and sat up, pulling one of the towels around him and tossing another towards Pippa.

'I don't believe this!' he muttered, barely concealing his indignation. 'That's the captain calling out to me. I asked him not to disturb us, so he wouldn't dare come over into our little bay.'

'But what is he saying?' Pippa asked as she watched Adonis leaping to his feet, hauling on his clothes impatiently.

'A radio message. Damn that radio! Why do I always have to be in touch with the outside world?'

'Is it the hospital?' Pippa asked, taking hold of Adonis's outstretched hand and pulling herself up. She began to run across the sand to where she'd cast off her uniform.

'No, the captain is calling out that my father is ill
. . .very ill. He may be dying.'

'Then you have to go to him, Adonis,' Pippa said,
fastening the buttons of her uniform dress.

She felt intensely incongruous dressed in uniform,
standing on a deserted beach, her skin tight with the
salt of the sea water and tingling with the excitement
of their unconsummated passion.

Adonis moved swiftly over the sand to cup her face
in his hands. 'But you wanted me. . .as much as I
wanted you, Pippa. Remember that feeling, and when
I come back from Athens——'

'From Athens!' Pippa repeated. She had forgotten
how far away Adonis's father was. She would have to
live without him again. Just when they were getting
back together again. Just when their problems seemed
to be receding.

Adonis took hold of her hand and pulled her along,
over the sand, to clamber over the rocks at the top of
their secret cove.

The captain of the boat was standing on deck, using
a loud hailer to repeat his message that Adonis must
return on board. Adonis went below to check the
radio. Pippa remained on deck, feeling suddenly
drained of all energy by the frustration of the situation.

Adonis came back on deck after a few minutes, his
face grim as he gave instructions to the crew.

'What's happened, Adonis?' Pippa asked as the boat
headed for Ceres again.

'My father is in a coma. He is not expected to live,'
Adonis replied in a flat tone. 'I have to go at once.'

They remained on deck, silently watching the
approaching shore.

As they reached Ceres again Adonis leaped ashore,

holding out his hand for Pippa. Neither of them spoke until they were at the top of the hill.

'I'll take you to the detox unit, Pippa,' Adonis said quietly. 'Dr Samos will arrange for a driver to take you back to hospital after your visit.'

He brought the Land Rover to a halt near the dense trees where they had lingered on their last visit together. As he switched off the engine he leaned across and brushed her lips with his own. The passion that had smouldered and threatened to burst into flames had been quenched by the unfortunate turn of events.

And then Adonis was jumping down from the Land Rover, moving swiftly to open the passenger door for her. He held her in his arms as her feet touched the ground, and she closed her eyes to savour the moment.

'Goodbye,' he whispered.

An intense feeling of loneliness swept over her as the Land Rover disappeared down the mountain road. She took a deep breath. She had to keep going, to throw herself into her work so that she had no time to worry about her own personal problems.

Dr Samos was waiting for her at the door of the detox unit. 'Welcome again, Sister Manson. I saw Dr Patras driving away. No doubt his duties——'

'His father is very ill, Dr Samos,' she said quietly. 'He has to go to Athens.'

'Ah, yes, his father. I hope he will be in time to effect a reconciliation,' the doctor replied.

Pippa frowned. It seemed everyone knew more about Adonis's life than she did. 'I wasn't aware that Dr Patras's rift with his father was common knowledge.'

'Oh, yes, indeed it is, among the Greeks who have

known Adonis since he was a young man. And I myself have been particularly affected by Adonis's quarrel with his father. If Adonis hadn't insisted that. . .' The psychiatrist broke off. 'I can see that Adonis hasn't confided in you, so I mustn't betray a confidence. Would you like some refreshment before we look around the unit?' Dr Samos asked.

Adonis certainly hadn't confided in her. She had no idea what Dr Samos was talking about. This was just another example of how much she stood on the outside. And as for confiding in her, Adonis had only told her the smallest details about his complicated life.

'No, thank you. Please show me round now, Dr Samos,' Pippa replied, summoning up her flagging interest in the project. The salt from the sea water on her skin was chafing against the cotton of the uniform dress and she was longing to get back to her room at the hospital and have a shower.

As she followed Dr Samos around the unit she was intensely aware that there had been preparations for her visit. There were only four patients visible. The rest had retired early to their own rooms.

'I believe I told you on your last visit that we have some sensitive patients whose identity we keep secret,' Dr Samos told her. 'As administrative sister of the hospital you have every right to meet them, but they would prefer not to see you. They have come to trust the staff up here, but any new face is regarded with suspicion; however, if you wish—'

'No, no, of course not. I wouldn't dream of invading the privacy of their rooms,' Pippa put in quickly. 'I understand the situation perfectly.'

She listened to Dr Samos extolling the virtues of their method, which was to use as few drugs as possible. Suitable patients would eliminate all drug-taking and rely only on counselling.

'But isn't this rather drastic?' Pippa asked. 'Aren't the withdrawal symptoms severe with the "cold turkey" method?'

Dr Samos nodded. 'Yes, indeed. That is why my patients need expert counselling. But I have discovered over the years that introducing milder drug substances like methadone in an effort to wean the patient creates more problems than it solves. Often the patient becomes hooked on methadone and the vicious cycle starts up again. Far better to rely on professional counselling from myself and my colleagues and group therapy where appropriate.'

At the end of the visit, Pippa's head was spinning with the information Dr Samos had given her. She was no longer in any doubt that the worthy doctor was doing an excellent job at the detox unit. She decided to respect his call for a low-profile situation. If he had sensitive patients, then she wouldn't pry. After all, she had enough to do running the hospital. But she would have liked to know how Adonis's quarrel with his father had affected the detox unit and she wondered, fleetingly, if she would ever fully understand the complicated family background which seemed to dictate Adonis's life.

She thanked the doctor as he walked to the outside door at the end of her visit. A telephone call had summoned one of the hospital drivers with a car to the top of the hill. She shook the doctor's hand and walked across the narrow strip of dry grass that separated the unit from the stony hillside track.

The doctor closed the door and the velvet cloak of darkness enveloped her. As her eyes adjusted to the glimmer of the stars above her she remembered the last time she had stood up here in the moonlight.

The hospital driver was holding the door of the car open for her. Before she climbed inside she looked up at the stars for a brief moment of nostalgia. Tonight there was no shooting star to wish on. But would it have done any good even if there had been? She couldn't make the same wish again, especially when the likelihood of it ever coming true was fast receding.

CHAPTER ELEVEN

ADONIS returned from Athens a couple of weeks later in a subdued mood. Pippa sensed that at first he didn't want to discuss the events surrounding his time in the Patras family residence. It was only after several days that he opened up and told her what had happened.

'I stayed at my father's bedside, taking turns with my sister and my two brothers,' Adonis said quietly. 'My father was drifting in and out of a coma. After a few days he began to show signs of recovery and then, after two weeks, he became fully conscious again. But as soon as he recognised me he asked the nurses to remove me from the room.'

'No!' gasped Pippa.

She and Adonis were sitting in her office at the end of a morning during which Pippa had cleared away the backlog of her administration letters. Adonis had arrived just as Elena was leaving, so they were alone.

'But what a cruel thing to do after you had kept your bedside vigil for two weeks!' Pippa said. 'Surely your father's mind must have been affected by his illness.'

Adonis shook his head. 'No, my father is a very tough character. I knew he wouldn't want me there if he came round. But I had to be there in case he died. Family is family; he is my father and as such I must honour him.'

Pippa sat very still in her chair, feeling once more that she didn't understand Adonis. How could he speak so calmly of a man who refused to have him in the same room? Surely this was taking honour too far, especially when so much was at stake. . .like his own freedom to live his life in the way he wanted to.

She stood up. 'I have to go and discharge Chrisanthe,' she said gently. 'Giorgios, her husband, is coming to take her home at twelve. Nick Seferis has been well enough to work part-time while you were away, but I only call him out when there's no one else available.'

'I'll come with you,' Adonis said. 'I need to get back into harness. The inactivity of the last two weeks has been excruciating.'

Since his return Adonis had been withdrawn, curt to the point of rudeness. Pippa wondered if something else had happened while he was in Athens, something to change him.

There was a knock on the door and Ariadne Stangos came in.

'Chrisanthe is waiting for you, Sister,' she announced, glancing from one to the other with a benign smile.

'I know, and I'm on my way,' Pippa replied, wondering why Ariadne had needed to come along to her office when she could have picked up the internal phone.

'How was Athens, Dr Patras?' Ariadne persisted glibly. 'Cassiopi certainly seems to have done a lot of shopping while you were there. I love that new cream linen suit. Did you choose it together?'

Adonis's enigmatic expression gave nothing away. 'Always ready to gossip, aren't you?'

'So Cassiopi has returned from America, has she, Ariadne?' Pippa put in quickly, her voice coming out in an unrecognisable quaver of emotion. She kept her back deliberately turned towards Adonis, not wanting to witness his attempt at a denial.

'Oh, yes; she came back with Adonis from Athens. Didn't he tell you? They had lunch together yesterday at the Olympic Hotel — in a private room, so I hear — and I happened to see Cassiopi getting into her car in this fabulous new suit afterwards. She told me she'd bought it in her favourite boutique in Athens and that — '

'That's enough, Ariadne,' Adonis cut in. 'I thought we agreed to cut the gossip while we were on duty.'

'On duty, yes, Adonis,' Pippa said evenly. 'But off duty Ariadne is free to tell me everything she knows.'

She looked up into Adonis's eyes and saw raw pain. Without a word he walked away from her and out through the open door. As her eyes caught Ariadne's she saw the look of triumph on her colleague's face. At last she'd shattered the romantic dream.

'Pippa, I'm sorry if — '

'Let's go and see our patient, Ariadne,' Pippa broke in quickly. She had no desire to hear her worst fears voiced. She didn't feel strong enough to take it at the moment. She'd heard that time healed. Well, maybe in time she would get used to the fact that she'd fallen for the wrong man.

Ariadne remained quiet as they walked along the corridor to the obstetrics and gynaecology unit. Chrisanthe was sitting in a chair, her bag already packed, her husband looking fondly down at her. Adonis was also there, giving his professional advice on the after-care of his patient.

Pippa took a deep breath as she listened in.

'Not too much work at home. Chrisanthe must rest.

We won't expect her back here for at least three
months, but she will be paid for her sick-leave. I'd like
to see her once a week in Out-patients. The first
appointment will be next Monday morning at ten.'

Adonis paused as he handed over the appointment
card. He tensed as he realised that Pippa and Ariadne
were now in the room. 'And there's no reason why
you shouldn't try for another baby if you want one,'
he continued after a few seconds. 'Chrisanthe is in
good shape internally and the remaining fallopian tube
is healthy.'

A shy look passed between Chrisanthe and her
young husband.

'Giorgios has decided to come home for good,
Doctor. He will work as a waiter until we can afford
to buy our own little shop.'

Adonis smiled. 'Good. So you will have more time
together. That's what marriage is all about.'

Watching him, Pippa felt the full strength of her
loss. Adonis, by not denying that Cassiopi and he had
been together in Athens, had compounded his guilt.
But Pippa still loved him. She couldn't stop loving
him, whatever lies he'd told her. She couldn't kill off
her love at one fell swoop. It would take time before
the full realisation of her loss had sunk in.

She moved quickly forward to stand beside
Chrisanthe.

'Take care of yourself, Chrisanthe. We'll see you in
Out-patients next week and I shall look forward to
seeing you back on duty when. . .'

She paused, realising that she didn't know where
she would be in three months' time, but it certainly
wouldn't be on the island of Ceres.

'That is, the staff here will be delighted to welcome

you back. I expect Sister Arama will be in charge again.'

A shadow of a frown fell over Chrisanthe's face. 'I wish you were staying on, Sister Manson. You've been so helpful to me. Couldn't you change your mind?'

Pippa's skin felt as if it would crack when she smiled down at her patient, this young nurse who had caused her problems during the first weeks of her administration.

'My contract finishes in October, Chrisanthe. I shall be returning to London.'

As she looked up she was aware that Adonis was watching her with an enigmatic expression. She met his gaze unflinchingly. He had put her through a lot of pain, but she wouldn't have missed it for anything. It was part of living, a part she would never forget. And when the pain of longing had subsided she would remember him with affection.

'Sister Manson! Just a moment!'

Adonis was calling her back, but she pretended not to notice as she walked away down the corridor.

'We have to talk.' Adonis was now beside her, adjusting his long strides to her own.

She shook her head as she increased her pace. 'Oh, no, we've done all the talking we're going to do.'

'I won't hurt you, Pippa.' Adonis's hand touched her arm.

She flinched from the exquisite pleasure that contact with him gave her. This time his touch felt like a first-degree burn.

She turned to look up at him. 'No, you won't hurt me, Adonis, because you won't touch me again, either physically or emotionally. I'll stay on for my final weeks here and perform my duties to the best of my ability, but our personal relationship is over.'

The tantalising fingers were removed from her arm. She heard but didn't see as Adonis walked away. When she looked up he had gone. She breathed in deeply to steady her nerves.

'Are you OK, Sister Manson?'

It was Dominic Varios, the young doctor who had been the protègè of the Capodistrias family and still regarded the house in Symborio Bay where he had been born and his mother worked as a cook as his home.

She looked up into the kindly eyes of the young man. 'Yes, I'm fine, Dominic. Just a little faint with the heat, I think. We must do something about getting air-conditioning in the whole hospital. If I put the wheels in motion we could have it installed by next summer. I was speaking to Dr Demetrius about it a few weeks ago and——'

'Yes, he told me,' Dominic interjected enthusiastically. 'He also said he hadn't seen enough of you this summer. You haven't been over to Symborio for ages. I tried to convince him that it was work that was keeping you away, but——'

'I'll have to come over more often,' she said quickly. 'It's true I've been busy, but often it's easier just to curl up in my room rather than make the journey across the water.'

'You only have to pick up the phone and ask me to take you over there,' Dominic persisted. 'Come this evening. It would please Dr Demetrius so much. He's not getting any younger, you know.'

Pippa smiled, the first genuine smile of the morning. 'Yes, I'd like that.'

'Six o'clock OK?'

Pippa nodded. 'Fine.' She needed to get away from the hospital, to put space between herself and that two-timing, impossible man.

For the next month she studiously avoided Adonis, except in a professional capacity. She spent more and more of her free time over at the house in Symborio Bay, much to the delight of old Dr Demetrius Capodistrias, who had come to regard her as the daughter he'd never had.

Pippa's cousin Nicole with her husband, Dr Alexander Capodistrias, and the three children, Mark, Richard and Laura, returned from America two weeks early at the beginning of October, and there was a happy reunion dinner at the house. The house was big enough to accommodate everyone, and Dr Demetrius persuaded Pippa that there was no need to return to her hospital room after dinner.

The old doctor looked around the dinner-table. 'You know I've come to enjoy the evenings when Pippa has come over to visit me,' he told his son and daughter-in-law. 'So just because you two have decided to return from your travels it doesn't mean I'm going to be deprived of Pippa's company. There's room in this house for all of us.'

Pippa glanced at Nicole and saw that she was smiling happily. Although her cousin was now in her early thirties she still retained the fresh look of a young girl. Her fair hair, pulled back from her face into a becoming chignon, contrasted with her tanned skin. There had been lots of leisure time over in the States, apparently, when Nicole and Alexander had taken their children sailing. The children, now safely tucked up in bed, had told Pippa all about it this evening, before she'd read them a bedtime story.

'Don't worry, Demetrius,' Nicole said. 'We're all hoping to see more of Pippa. In fact Alexander has been trying to persuade her to stay on.'

Pippa drew in her breath. She'd already said no, but she knew that Alexander sensed how sad she was to be leaving.

'It's only two weeks to the end of Pippa's contract, Father,' Alexander put in quickly. 'I wish she would change her mind. We need a good administrative sister, and Sister Arama, having enjoyed her freedom in the States, is insisting on retiring. We're going to be in a fix if Pippa leaves us.'

'But Nicole has said she'll go back to her old job,' Pippa countered, looking across the table at her cousin for support.

Nicole smiled. 'Only until a replacement can be found,' she said gently. 'The children need me. I know Eirene will look after them here——' she glanced affectionately at Dominic's mother, who was clearing away the plates, that indispensable cook-housekeeper who had been with the family since Alexander was a child '—but I hate being away from them all day.'

'I thought you enjoyed your work in the hospital, Philippa,' old Dr Demetrius said. 'I've had nothing but glowing reports about you.'

Pippa rose from the table. 'Yes, I've enjoyed my work. And you've all been wonderful to me. But I think it's time to go back to England. I'm going to spend some time at home with my parents and then I'll probably look for a sister's post in the north of

England. Maybe at the cottage hospital where I used to work before I started my training.'

'So you're not going back to London?' Nicole asked.

'No; I've already written to the Benington explaining that I won't be returning. And now, if you'll excuse me, I'd like to go to my room. I've had a long day in hospital and I'm very tired.'

'Of course, my dear,' Dr Demetrius said kindly, making a valiant attempt to raise his old body from the ornate carving chair at the head of the table.

As Pippa took a final glance around the table a lump rose in her throat. She would miss this new life when she returned to England. That was why she'd decided not to return to the Benington. She needed some time to herself to recover from the events of the past six months. She knew that the prying questions of her London colleagues would continually open up the wounds that she was trying to heal.

She glanced across at her cousin Nicole. You only had to look at the way Alexander treated his wife to see that they were blissfully happy. It was good to know that some hospital romances had a happy ending!

She climbed up the stairs slowly; she was desperately tired and she hoped she would be able to sleep, because there were so many nights when she tossed and turned and sleep evaded her. And whenever she drifted off she would invariably find herself in confrontation with Adonis. She could avoid him during the day, but at night he was constantly in her thoughts.

Eirene had turned down Pippa's bed and put on the soft bedside lamps and concealed lighting that made the room so cosy and welcoming at the end of the day. Pippa walked out on to the small balcony and looked out across the water of Symborio Bay. A light twinkled in one of the boats moored at the landing-stage. She heard the sound of voices. A light, tinkling sound — Cassiopi. . .and a deeper, masculine tone — Adonis.

They were coming ashore, walking along the landing-stage into the waiting Land Rover. Pippa heard the sound of the engine starting up.

'Isn't it cold out on the balcony, Pippa?'

Pippa turned at the sound of Nicole's voice. Reluctantly she went back into her bedroom.

'Not cold, deliciously fresh. The wind is only slight and I love the cool air at the end of the day.'

The sound of the Land Rover climbing the hill could be heard clearly. Nicole leaned back against the armchair by the window and scrutinised her cousin.

'It's Adonis, isn't it, Pippa?'

Pippa sank down on to the turned-back sheets. Her cousin knew her so well. They had been so very close when Pippa was small. Nicole, being eight years older than she was, had been very helpful when Pippa was growing up. Why did she find it so hard to confide in her now? This was still the same psuedo-big-sister she'd grown up with.

'Is it so obvious?' Pippa countered.

'We're been home three days and you've never once mentioned his name. Whenever I phoned you from the States you were always talking about him. At first you seemed to positively hate him when he considered you wouldn't be fit enough for the job. But then, little by little, I could tell that you'd fallen for him. . . No, let me finish,' Nicole insisted, as Pippa tried to speak. 'I suppose you didn't dare tell me outright, over the phone, that you were in love with Adonis, in case someone was listening in at the switchboard.'

'I think you're imagining a lot of this,' Pippa said tonelessly. Opening up the wounds wasn't doing her any good at all. She'd come to terms with the situation . . .at least she thought she had.

'No, I'm not imagining it,' Nicole said firmly. 'I knew right from the first day I phoned you that there was some kind of love-hate relationship developing between you. I discussed it with Alexander and——'

'Oh, Nicole, you didn't!'

'I had to know why Adonis was being so hard on you when you first arrived. He's normally a very compassionate man,' Nicole hurried on, ignoring Pippa's interruption. 'Alexander told me that soon after Adonis became a consultant he appointed an agency nurse during a staff shortage. One night he left her in charge of a cardiac patient who was in an oxygen tent. The nurse, who was recovering from a car crash in which she'd suffered concussion three months before, blacked out during her course of night duty and the oxygen cylinder ran out. The first Adonis knew about it was when a distraught nursing sister phoned him. The sister had gone in to see the cardiac patient and found the nurse unconscious on the floor and the patient suffocating in the non-oxygenated tent. Adonis hurried over and was only just in time to save the patient's life. I think the experience affected him more than we thought.'

'How awful!' Pippa clasped her hand over her mouth in horror. 'And the nurse?' she asked quietly.

'She spent the next three months in hospital, undergoing tests, before spending a year in convalescence. Apparently she had sustained a hairline fracture of the skull at the time of the crash and this had never been picked up by the attending casualty officer.

Alexander told me that ever since that unfortunate incident Adonis has been wary of medical staff with any history of illness or injury. If I'd known this I certainly wouldn't have asked you to come out, Pippa. So you see I feel partly responsible for your ordeal.'

'It wasn't an ordeal, Nicole,' Pippa said, a wistful note creeping into her voice. 'I wouldn't have missed it for anything.'

'I know you wouldn't. But when we got back here Dominic told me he was worried about you. He said you and Adonis had seen a lot of each other and then the whole thing had stopped suddenly. . .soon after Adonis had been over to Athens to see his father. Did you have an affair. . .? I wouldn't blame you. I mean he's so gorgeous, absolutely your type, and——'

'Nicole, he's going to be married. . .to Cassiopi. I thought everyone knew that. He's not free to——'

'Pippa, you don't understand what goes on over here. Adonis is tied to. . .' Nicole hesitated. 'Adonis is tied to a promise made to his father. But it's only a question of time before he will be free.'

'You sound just like Adonis. . ."Only a question of time. . .let's play the waiting game"!' Pippa burst out. 'Well, this little girl has had enough of waiting. I'm getting out while I'm still young enough to enjoy myself.'

Nicole's eyes flickered. 'You must do as you think best for you, but I think you're making a mistake. When I met Alexander we went through all sorts of trauma before we could be together. The path of true love is never easy, but it's worth sticking it out until you've overcome the problems.'

'But how can I overcome the problem if I don't

know what it is? What is this promise Adonis has made to his father?'

Nicole drew in her breath. 'I can't tell you, because I don't fully understand it myself. I know it involves the Manoulis and the Patras families. There is a great deal at stake and Adonis knows this. He is a very honourable man; he would never jeopardise the honour of his family.'

'But Ariadne told me that——'

'Oh, Ariadne!' Nicole uttered the name scornfully. 'An excellent nursing sister, but her personal life is now so boring that she has to poke her nose in other people's. But what would gall her the most would be the way you and Adonis were getting on together. You see, she's always fancied her chances with Adonis, ever since they were young. And Adonis has refused to take her seriously. They say hell has no fury like a woman scorned. If Ariadne can't have him no one else can. I'm sure she must realise that the betrothal between Adonis and Cassiopi is a sham, but yet she——'

'Then it really is a sham?'

Nicole bridled. 'I shouldn't have said that. . .not until. . .but we shall know soon enough. A conference of the two families has been called in Athens. That's why Cassiopi and Adonis were making their way up to the Manoulis house just now. . .to help Cassiopi's father to prepare for the journey tomorrow.'

'And where will the conference take place?'

'At the bedside of Adonis's father. It's now recognised that he has only days to live. Alexander has been asked to go as some kind of mediator.'

'And will Adonis go to this mysterious conference?'

Nicole shook her head. 'As you probably know, his

father refused to allow him to stay at his bedside when
he was ill, a few weeks ago.'

'That's sad, so very sad. . .'

Pippa broke off at the sound of the returning Land
Rover. There was a squeal of brakes, followed by the
scrunch of gravel, and then voices below them.

She went out on to the balcony. The security light at
the front of the house lit up the figure of Adonis
climbing out of the Land Rover. . .alone. Pippa's
heart began to beat faster.

He was walking along the jetty towards the waiting
boat. She longed to call him back, but she was too
proud. To proud and too confused. She didn't know
what she should believe any more.

CHAPTER TWELVE

IT WAS Pippa's last day at the hospital. She looked around the little office that she had come to regard with such affection. Elena was making no disguise of the fact that she was unhappy at Pippa's leaving them.

'I know it will be nice to work with Sister Nicole again, but that's only a temporary situation,' the kindly medical secretary moaned. 'And we don't know who we'll get to replace you. Sister Ariadne put in for the job, but she wasn't even short-listed. When you've grown up in a community people don't take you seriously. And anyway, she hasn't got enough paper qualifications.'

And she talks too much! Pippa would have liked to say, but didn't. The rift between herself and the gynaecology and obstetrics sister had been healed, but they'd agreed to avoid all gossip. Pippa had even started helping with the feeds occasionally and had insisted that the conversation be strictly professional.

'It's good to see Dr Capodistrias back in Greece again,' Elena said, 'if only for a short time, before he goes off again on another lecture tour. This time it's in Hong Kong. Tell me, Sister, when does he come back from the Manoulis-Patras family conference in Athens?'

Pippa shook her head. 'I've no idea. The funeral of Stamatis Patras was yesterday, so maybe he'll return today.'

'Perhaps Dr Patras will return with him.'

'Perhaps,' Pippa said lightly.

The events of the past week had been a complete mystery to her. She had been assisting Adonis in Theatre at the beginning of the week and a call had come through that he was to fly to Athens immediately. His father was asking for him.

'Asking for me?' Adonis had repeated.

And Pippa and the rest of the surgical team were amazed to see the surgeon throw his surgical cap into the air and give out a loud whoop of joy. Then, remembering where he was, he'd asked Pippa to find a clean cap and refix his very unsterile black locks beneath it. They were fortunately at the suture stage, otherwise Pippa was sure someone else would have had to take over.

Adonis had left the hospital immediately after the operation was finished. And two days later had come the news of his father's death. She hoped and prayed that there had been a reconciliation between father and son.

'I've got to help Nick Seferis in Out-patients,' she told Elena. 'Sister Demotis has to go off at twelve and Sister Stangos is specialling a difficult gynae case. So I said I'd do the last hour before lunch.'

Elena nodded. 'I'll get the letters typed up for you to sign this afternoon, Sister. . .the last time. . .'

Pippa felt a pang of regret as she watched the secretary retreat to her little room beside Pippa's office. She was going to miss her. . . She was going to miss everything about this hospital. . .especially. . .

Determinedly she refused to think about him as she walked quickly down the corridor towards Out-patients. Pushing open the doctors' office door, she went in. 'Dr Seferis, I. . .'

But it wasn't Nick Seferis sitting at the desk.

'Adonis! I didn't know you were back.'

'I got back mid-morning and came in to find that Nick was feeling a bit tired, so I volunteered to take over. I'm glad you came in, because I can tell you the good news about our patient here.'

Pippa looked down at the young woman on the examination couch.

'Hello, Chrisanthe,' she said to the patient who had survived the difficult ectopic operation. 'How are you?'

Chrisanthe smiled. 'I'm fine. Wait till Dr Patras tells you the news.'

Sister Demotis was taking off her apron, preparing to leave. 'Now that you've come, Sister Manson, I'll go off duty.'

Pippa nodded. 'Yes, of course. Now about this news. . .'

Adonis smiled. 'I've just examined Chrisanthe; her period is only two weeks overdue, but she couldn't wait to see if she was pregnant. Her urine test is positive and the clinical signs are all there in the uterus, so. . .'

'That's great! Well done, Chrisanthe.'

'Will you be here when I have the baby? I heard that Sister Arama has decided to retire,' Chrisanthe said.

'No, I won't be here, I'm afraid,' Pippa said quickly. 'But I'm sure whoever takes over after Sister Nicole Capodistrias leaves will make you very comfortable.'

Adonis was washing his hands at the sink. Pippa busied herself reorganising the examination trolley and studiously avoided looking across at him.

Chrisanthe announced that she was dressed and Pippa pulled back the curtain from the cubicle. She went in, stripped the couch, and changed the sheet. Chrisanthe lingered on.

'Thanks for everything, Sister. Giorgios and I have decided to call our baby Adonis if it's a boy and Philippa if it's a girl. I hope you don't mind.'

'Mind?' Pippa and Adonis spoke in unison and then both paused in an awkward silence. Adonis was the first to resume conversation.

'Well, I for one will be delighted. How about you, Philippa?'

She smiled. 'It will be good to know I'm remembered out here.'

'Go and tell your husband the good news,' Adonis said. 'And I'll see you again next week, same time. Got to keep an eye on my special patient.'

Pippa watched Chrisanthe moving away as if she were floating on a cloud. That was the second happy ending today. The first had been Geoffrey, who'd been allowed to leave hospital and move next door to his own little flat. Gina, looking like a round little barrel, had welcomed her husband home with open arms, and Geoffrey had joked that it was almost impossible now for him to put his arms around his wife.

There were only three more patients to see before the end of the morning. As soon as the final patient left, Pippa began to clear up the treatment-room, supervising the two junior nurses who were helping her. Adonis was sorting through the case-files, adding extra messages into his dictaphone for Elena to transcribe. He obviously didn't need her help or he would have called her over. Soon he wouldn't need her at all. But maybe she ought to check. . .just in case.

'Do you need any help, Dr Patras?'

Adonis opened his mouth, but before he could reply

the swing-doors of Out-patients burst open and Geoffrey stood there, panting for breath.

'Why, Geoffrey, what on earth —— ?' Pippa began.

'It's Gina. She's having rapid contractions. She didn't tell you this morning that she was having awful backache because she thought you wouldn't let me come home. But now her waters have broken.'

'Where is she?'

'She's still at home. . .in the flat. . .refusing to leave. She wants the baby to be born in our own home. That's why she was hanging on so long without telling anybody.'

'Oh, Gina, Gina!' Pippa muttered under her breath. 'After we'd agreed that she would come in as soon as. . . Never mind, it doesn't matter now. The main thing is to make it a safe delivery.'

Geoffrey stood awkwardly, holding on to his stick, one hand rubbing down the side of his injured leg. 'Then you'll come back to the flat with me?'

'Of course!' Adonis was already gathering up the necessary equipment. 'If there are no complications we'll deliver the baby just how Gina wants it. After all, women have been having babies in their own homes since the beginning of time.'

Pippa flashed him a grateful smile. She'd thought Adonis might have been a stickler for technology, but no, she'd found him to be very human where delivering babies was concerned. And he never complained about the sometimes weird requests the mothers made when *in extremis*.

'I'll hobble on behind you,' Geoffrey said. 'You'll get there quicker than me.'

* * *

Gina was lying on the bed in her little flower-filled flat, panting hard.

'I'm doing everything. . .you. . .told me. . . Sister,' she said, between breaths.

'Everything except come into hospital,' Pippa said with a wry smile.

Gina attempted to smile, but screwed up her face at the beginning of another contraction. 'I suddenly thought how nice it would be if. . .if. . . Hold my hand, Sister. And make Geoffrey sit down when he gets here. He's a bit squeamish and I don't want him to faint.'

Adonis made a quick examination. There had been no complications during the routine antenatal examination two days before, so he wasn't expecting there to be any problem with this birth.

'Gina, you can push now,' Adonis said.

Gina looked excited as she squeezed Pippa's hand. 'Won't be. . .long. . .noowowow. . .'

'Pant now,' Pippa said, as Adonis signalled that the head was crowning.

She moved quickly to stand beside Adonis as the head and the face were slowly delivered.

'Check the umbilical cord,' Adonis said quickly.

Pippa leaned forward and slid a gloved finger under the pubic arch until she had located the cord and moved it out of harm's way.

The next contraction completed delivery of the shoulders and body and then the entire little infant slithered out and began bawling its tiny head off.

'No problem with the lungs!' Adonis smiled as he placed the infant in the proud mother's arms. 'You've got a little boy.'

'Adonis!' the mother said, and she wasn't referring to her doctor.

Geoffrey stood up from the chair in which he'd been rooted during the entire proceedings. Rather shakily he walked the few steps to his wife's bedside. 'Well done, Gina,' he murmured before turning white and slipping backwards against Adonis.

Adonis helped him back into his chair. 'It's always harder for the father,' Adonis said with a wry grin. 'Take care of Gina, Sister, while I check the baby over.'

An hour later Adonis insisted that Gina and Geoffrey should allow the nurses and doctors to come in and out of the flat as necessary for the first few days. And he'd also persuaded the proud parents that they should contact their own parents in England and tell them about their new grandson.

'They'll probably want to come out and visit you when they hear the news,' Pippa said. 'You'd be surprised how a new baby can heal a family rift.'

Gina smiled contentedly. 'You're probably right, Sister. The main thing is that they'll see that Geoffrey and I are so happy together.'

'I'll make all the arrangements with the medical staff who're going to look after you for the first few days,' Adonis said. 'But you can go now, Sister.'

He was already picking up the phone. She wasn't needed any more.

Pippa walked out into the hot afternoon sunshine. She'd just scrubbed her hands at the sink, and she held them out towards the sun to dry. Suddenly she felt lost. The activity of the last few hours had kept her from thinking about anything except the patients, but now. . .

She walked slowly across the little courtyard towards
her room. She didn't want to go inside and finish her
packing. She didn't want to be alone with her thoughts.
She would sit in the sun. . .just this one last time,
before. . .

Even with her eyes closed, she recognised Adonis's
step. His tall frame obliterated the rays of the sun. She
opened her eyes and looked up at him.

'I thought you were organising the obstetrics team,'
she began.

'It's done. I'll go back later. I wanted to see you
before you go.'

'Well, sit down,' she said unsteadily.

'Not here. What I have to say must be said in
private. So shall we go to my room or yours?'

'Mine,' she said quickly. It was nearer and she felt
more confident on home territory. If there was to be a
show-down. . .

She pushed open the door and sat down at the seat
beside her desk. Her case lay open, half packed on the
bed. Adonis moved it to one side and perched on the
edge. It was as if they were two strangers.

'Did you manage to have a reconciliation with your
father before. . .before he died?' she asked gently.

For a moment she saw a haze across Adonis's eyes.
He moved a hand and wiped cautiously at his eyelids.
When he spoke his voice was husky.

'Such a waste, the years when we hardly ever spoke
to each other. Yes, he asked to see me, as you know.
He told me he regretted that we'd been estranged for
so long.'

'But why was this?'

Adonis hesitated before taking a deep, rasping
breath. His voice when he spoke was low and strained.

'You have to understand the family background. My grandfather was a poor fisherman, but my father had big ideas. He saw that honest toil wouldn't give him the material possessions he longed for, so he turned to crime. He became involved in drug smuggling, first as a courier and then, when he became richer, he bought his own ship, later many ships, and transported drugs under the cover of his new-found respectability. He changed his name and the authorities never knew that Stamatis Patras had been in prison as a youth.'

Pippa remained still and calm, not wanting to break the spell of fascination that had descended on her.

Adonis stood up and walked across the room, standing beside the window, his face half shaded from Pippa's eyes as he continued his story.

'When I was very small my mother told me the truth about my father and begged me to do something useful with my life. I was with her the day she died when my little brother was stillborn. I was only twelve, but I decided then to become a doctor so that I could help rather than hinder the progress of mankind.'

He broke off and turned to give Pippa a gentle smile. 'It sounds pompous, but that was my wish when I was twelve.'

'And you made the wish come true,' she said gently, feeling a surge of admiration for the child Adonis.

'Yes, but in the meantime my father's fleet was being investigated. Palms were greased, but it was the testimony of his old friend, Stavros Manoulis, Cassiopi's father, that saved him from exposure. The drug trading was stopped; at least, that's what everyone thought. But, growing up in my father's house, I knew otherwise. Just before I went off to medical school I had a long discussion with my father. I told him that, as a future doctor, I couldn't condone what he was doing and I would expose his activities if he didn't promise to stop. I also added another condition . . .that he should set up a trust fund to help finance worthwhile medical projects. I was able to help with the founding of the drug rehabilitation centre here on Ceres, and there have been many other projects over the years. But my father bore me a grudge, even though he agreed that his illegal activities had to stop.'

The pieces of the puzzle were beginning to fall into place. 'So that's what Dr Samos meant when he mentioned that your quarrel with your father had an effect on him,' Pippa murmured. 'But when he saw that you hadn't explained the situation to me he didn't elaborate. But tell me, what did you discuss at the family conference? I mean, if the drug activities had stopped all those years ago and——'

'We agreed to break off the betrothal agreement between Cassiopi and myself.'

Adonis moved across the room and stood looking down at her.

She held her breath. 'But you weren't even invited to the conference at first.'

'No, but Cassiopi was. She was going to plead on my behalf. You see, it was at my instigation that the betrothal took place in the first place. About five years ago Cassiopi's father had a disagreement with mine. They were old friends, but they could be very stubborn with each other. Stavros Manoulis uttered the ultimate threat. . . He said he was going to expose my father's earlier drug activities. He said he was sorry he'd covered up for him. Anyway, while all the mud was being slung around, Cassiopi and I got our heads together to try and find a solution. We'd always been great friends, but in a brother and sister sort of way. I came up with the idea that if we got betrothed and made it look as if we were going to get married and produce the next generation of Patras-Manoulis children the fathers would stop arguing. The Patras family name would be saved, because Stavros Manoulis wouldn't want his daughter married into a family of doubtful background. And we knew it was only temporary, because my father's terminal cancer had already been diagnosed. All we had to do was play the waiting game.'

'The waiting game,' Pippa breathed, as a light began to dawn. 'So the betrothal really was a sham.'

'As I told you,' he said evenly. 'Cassiopi is already on her way back to the States to rejoin her lover. She spent all her time in Athens shopping for her trousseau.'

Pippa drew in her breath. 'There's something else that's been explained to me, Adonis. I hadn't realised that your treatment of me when I first arrived wasn't personal. . . Yes, Nicole told me about your bad experience with the medically unfit nurse.'

He ran a hand through his tousled black hair. 'It's taken me a long time to get over it. . . I suppose you've helped by showing me that not all injured nurses are a liability. It's a pity you've got to go. We would have made a great team, you and I. Alexander has asked me to stay on. He's taking on more and more of this academic work, while I'm heavily into returning to real medicine. I'm going to resign my academic post in Athens. After my bad experience with the injured nurse I jumped at the chance of joining the sterile, well ordered life of a professor. But now I'm finding a great satisfaction in getting back to grass roots, working among real people. . .but sailing off on my boat in the afternoons with a beautiful girl beside me. . .'

He was hauling her to her feet, his eyes betraying his amusement at her puzzled expression. She tensed as she felt his arms around her waist.

'Adonis, I'm going back to England. Your dream may have come true, but——'

'No, it hasn't. Because there's no dream without you, Pippa. Surely you understand that. The waiting game's over and we're free to love each other. Marry me, Pippa. Stay out here with me forever. We'll start our own family; we'll——'

'Hold on, Adonis!' She didn't know whether she was laughing or crying. 'One thing at a time. What was the first idea?'

'Marriage. . .as soon as possible. In the beautiful church of Ayios Nicolas. The whole island will want to come. Oh, Pippa, say yes. I love you so much.'

His arms were tightening around her waist. She raised her face towards his and he kissed her, gently at first and then with an intensity and passion that grew stronger. He lifted her into his arms and carried her over to the bed, pushing the half-packed case on to the floor. . .

Much later, as they surfaced amid the rumpled sheets, Adonis said, 'Was that a yes or no?'

Pippa glanced around at the floor, strewn with the remnants of her packing. 'I suppose I'd better say yes. It would be too much trouble to start packing now. I'll have to cancel my flight and make a phone call home to my parents. I expect Mum will forgive me for changing my plans if there's a wedding in the offing.'

'Stop being so practical,' Adonis said, reaching for her again. 'You'll have to persuade me you're really going to marry me. I'm not totally convinced. . .'

Discover the thrill of *Love on Call* with 4 FREE Romances

FREE
BOOKS FOR YOU

In the exciting world of modern medicine, the emotions of true love acquire an added poignancy. Now you can experience these gripping stories of passion and pain, heartbreak and happiness - with Mills & Boon absolutely FREE! AND look forward to a regular supply of *Love on Call* delivered direct to your door.

🐾 🐾 🐾

Turn the page for details of how to claim 4 FREE books AND 2 FREE gifts!

An irresistible offer from Mills & Boon

Here's a very special offer from Mills & Boon for you to become a regular reader of *Love on Call*. And we'd like to welcome you with 4 books, a cuddly teddy bear and a special mystery gift - absolutely FREE and without obligation!

Then, every month look forward to receiving 4 brand new *Love on Call* romances delivered direct to your door for only £1.80 each. Postage and packing is FREE! Plus a FREE Newsletter featuring authors, competitions, special offers and lots more...

This invitation comes with no strings attached. You may cancel or suspend your subscription at any time and still keep your FREE books and gifts.

It's so easy. Send no money now but simply complete the coupon below and return it today to:

Mills & Boon Reader Service, FREEPOST, PO Box 236, Croydon, Surrey CR9 9EL.

— — — — — — — **NO STAMP NEEDED** — — — — — ✂

YES! Please rush me 4 FREE *Love on Call* books and 2 FREE gifts! Please also reserve me a Reader Service subscription. If I decide to subscribe, I can look forward to receiving 4 brand new *Love on Call* books for only £7.20 every month - postage and packing FREE. If I choose not to subscribe, I shall write to you within 10 days and still keep the FREE books and gifts. I may cancel or suspend my subscription at any time simply be writing to you.
I am over 18 years of age.   Please write in BLOCK CAPITALS

Ms/Mrs/Miss/Mr _____ EP62D

Address _____

_____

_____ Postcode _____

Signature _____

mps
MAILING
PREFERENCE
SERVICE

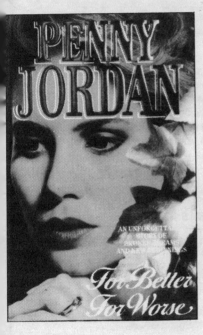

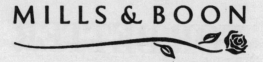